CW00820790

LAYLA'S

PAUL MCCRACKEN

CONTENTS

DEDICATION

Dedicated to my inspiration behind this book. My daughter, Ella

DAY ZERO

The screech of the alarm bell echoes throughout the factory, signalling the start of another shift. I make my way through the workshop, past the workers and the large, heavy machinery, to my office overlooking the factory.

I climb the steel stairs and enter the office which is sat above a freight container. The lights are already on and the other scheduler, Martin, is sat at his computer, opening up the programs. I pass him and take a seat at my computer and switch it on.

'Hey, David. Ready for another day of it?' Martin asks.

'Yep, is it the same mess with the London order?' I ask him.

'Of course, it is. I've been pressing Derek for more time, maybe another week.'

'Not for having it?' I ask.

'You know him, the date is the date. Would love to see him trying to fit it in, on top of all the rest we have going,' Martin says.

He slumps back in his chair, pointing at the time frames on his screen.

We print out the work schedules and go down to the workshop floor and hand them out to the guys.

The day is another high-pressured and busy one. It goes in quite quickly which is both good and bad. There are not enough hours in the day to complete the workload that the boys upstairs are calling for, but we can only work as fast as the machines allow us.

We punch out at four o'clock and I start the drive back home. The worst thing about winter is, when you start work it's dark and when you're heading home, it's dark again.

I live in a small town outside Belfast called Holywood. It is just past the George Best Belfast City Airport.

It takes me thirty minutes to get there. It is all motorway, the whole way there and back. In the rain, the spray from the road makes it almost impossible to see, like tonight. I rely on the tail lights of other drivers to guide my way as even the white lines of the road become blurry.

When I get home, I park in the driveway and turn off the engine. I lean over the passenger seat and pull down the sun visor to look in the mirror. I try to fix my short dark hair which has fallen flat in work. I also notice a couple of new wrinkles under my eyes, I've started to feel old ever since I turned thirty-four last month.

I get out and go inside the house.

When I open the door, I nearly slip on a plastic dog left laying near the doormat.

Layla leaving her toys in the hall again.

'Layla!' I call.

'Daddy!' I hear her small voice call back from somewhere upstairs.

'Come down and pick up your toys before dinner!' I call before I make my way to the kitchen, slinging my coat over one of the wooden chairs of the dining table.

At the kitchen counter, Lisa is chopping carrots. It's always her brown streaked hair that makes her stand out. If she were lost in a crowd, it'd always be my way of finding her.

She recently got it done for our anniversary, I pay for it every year. I walk up behind her and cuddle her.

'What do you want?' she sighs.

'Nothing, just cuddling ya.'

'Mmm, what have you done?' she asks.

'I haven't done anything, why do you always assume I've done something when I'm just being nice?'

'Cos you're never nice.'

'Oh, I'm never nice?' I ask, playfully.

'C'mon, piss off. I'm chopping here unless you want me to chop something else?' she says as she raises the knife for me to see.

I let go of her and go to the fridge to take out a drink.

'Can you not wait? Dinner is nearly ready,' Lisa says.

She's done her make up well tonight as if she were heading out somewhere. She has soft round cheeks that always seem slightly blushed. Lovely round brown eyes and smooth but thin lips that she always tries to bulk up with the deepest colour palettes of lipstick.

'Nope,' I say bluntly as I open the can and start to drink.

Layla comes in, still in her school uniform and hugs me. She recently turned five in January. When she stands straight, her head is up past my elbow, she's going to be taller than me in a few years. She has her mum's brown eyes and my dark hair. She has a really cute face, especially when she smiles.

'Did mummy tell you what I did in school today?' Layla asks.

'No, she didn't.

'She pulls on a badge on her jumper to show me. 'I'm class captain this week,' she says proudly.

'Wow, that's good, well done,' I tell her.

We all sit down and have dinner together. Lisa has made the usual potatoes, mince and vegetables. In the middle of dinner, the house phone starts to ring. I rise out of my seat to go to it but Lisa is first to her feet.

'Sit down and eat, I'll get it,' she says.

I sit back down.

Layla looks straight at me and starts to smile. I raise my fork to hers. We start hitting them off each other like swords. She smiles even wider and starts to make grunting noises, trying harder to stab me now.

'No! Yes, I'm sure!' I hear Lisa's voice raise in the hall. I stop playing with the forks.

'Beat ya!' Layla says, but my focus is completely on the phone conversation.

'Who are you to threaten me?' Lisa's voice rages.

I get out of my seat and go into the hall as she slams the phone down.

'Who was that?' I ask.

'Some asshole who got the wrong number,' she says, clearly upset.

'You OK?'

'I'm fine. Go finish your dinner,' she says, running her hand through her hair and then down the side of her face.

I stay up later than usual as everyone else goes to bed.

I sit up watching old films. I've watched them a hundred times over but for some reason they never age. I know what's going to happen but it doesn't take away from the quality of the story.

4

My eyes start to hurt and fail me so I decide to call it a night.

I double-check all of the doors are locked and glance out of the windows through the blinds.

The street looks empty.

I take the rubbish from the kitchen to the outside bin as an excuse to check outside, to listen. I dump the rubbish in the big black bin out in the back garden and pause for a second.

Taking in any sound that I can.

Everything sounds quiet and peaceful.

Once I get to the bedroom, Lisa is fast asleep, spread out and taking up most of the bed. I peer out the window through the closed curtains at the street below, still empty, still quiet. I get into bed, restless and anxious, trying my best to fall asleep.

***

Today, I'm completely snowed under with orders in work. Spending most of my time in the office trying to draft schedules to suit the shipping dates.

It's around ten in the morning and I'm just about to take a break when my phone rings. It's an unknown number. I hate answering unknown numbers. Most of the time it's a telemarketer trying to claim that you were in a car crash or whether you would benefit from a new service provider. I decide to answer anyway, just to see who it is.

'Hello?'

'Michael, we've been trying to reach you,' a cold voice says.

I stand up and go to the door, Martin watches me as I leave the office. I go down the stairs and out a fire door to the side of the building to get quiet and privacy.

'Who is this?'

'You know who it is. That wife of yours has quite a mouth on her.'

'You've got the wrong number, I don't know what you're talking about.'

'Michael, what happened to the drop?'

'Drop? What drop? I don't know what you're talking about, my name is David Isaac.'

'Don't fuck with me, Michael. I heard you had a little girl with that whore, Lisa.'

'You stay the fuck away from my family!' I shout, losing my temper.

'There's the one I'm looking for, glad you're still there. Now, tell me what you did with the drop or—'

I hang up.

I spend a couple of moments outside, looking at my phone to see if they call back, as well as having the time to calm down. I go back inside and back to the office.

I spend the remainder of the day with the phone right beside my computer so I don't miss a call or a message. Nervously switching my gaze from the monitor to the phone's screen every few minutes.

I'm in more of a rush home than usual. I need to make sure Lisa and Layla are safe.

Once I get home, Layla is helping Lisa peel the potatoes. My nerves eased a bit at the sight of them.

I walk up the hall into the kitchen.

Layla turns and sees me.

'Look, mummy showed me how to peel,' she says.

'You're doing a good job,' I tell her.

'You okay?' Lisa asks, obviously spotting something in my voice.

'Yeah, I'm fine, just the pressure I'm under in work. I'm a bit tired.'

'Did you get the sausages on your way home?' she asks.

I completely forgot that she texted me to get them on the way home tonight.

'No, I forgot all about them. I'll pop round the garage now. It'll only take me five minutes.

'Okay, get the big chunky ones,' she says.

'Okay,' I say as I dig out my car keys from my coat and leave the house again.

I take the five-minute drive to the garage on the edge of the town. I get the sausages and I am just about to get into the car when my phone starts ringing in my pocket. I take it out, it's Lisa.

'Hey.'

'David! Some men are trying to get into the house.'

'What? Lock the doors.'

'I locked them when I saw them coming up our drive.'

I hear loud banging in the background.

'Oh god, they're kicking the door, David! Me and Layla are under our bed,' She says on the brink of tears.

I drop the sausages and jump into the car. 'I'm coming now! I'm coming!'

I throw the phone on the passenger seat and race out of the garage forecourt.

I hear Lisa's whimpered cries coming from the phone in the passenger seat as I race through the streets to get home.

I hear a loud scream and I stomp the accelerator to the floor.

I pull up outside the house and sprint inside.

The front door has been kicked in.

I enter the hall.

'Lisa! Lisa!' I call out.

I hear cries coming from upstairs. I run up them as quick as I can and go into our bedroom to find her sitting on the bed. I go over to her. Tears stream her face as she sobs uncontrollably.

'Where's Layla?' I ask her repeatedly.

She looks up and I can see that her face is bruised.

'Lisa, where's Layla?' I ask again, more aggressively losing my patience.

'They took her,' she says blankly.

I turn and leave the room. 'Layla?' I cry out, hoping to hear a sweet voice replying.

I check her room.

The door is already open but inside is empty, the soft glow of her tiny lamp shows the emptiness of her bed.

I dart to the bathroom, even checking behind the shower curtain in a state of wishful but irrational thinking.

I scramble down the stairs again and then out to the back garden, my heart racing with a cold shiver remaining constant in my veins, no signs of anyone. I go back out to my car, not even closing the front door behind me. I get into it and take off at full speed, checking the nearby streets.

I spend the next hour scanning the streets for any suspicious activity or signs of Layla or her captors. I pin

8

hope on every passing figure I encounter on my way but none of them turns out to be Layla.

The dimly lit streets and darkened woodland areas make my search even more difficult and confusing as to whether I should get out and check certain spots that seem like they could be hiding something. But I know time is critical at this moment. She gets further and further from my reach with every passing second, and I know it.

I can't afford to waste any time searching in the wrong spot.

I drive, and I keep driving, I can't stop, I can't give up on my little girl. I even turn to interrogating night staff at the petrol stations that I pass, praying for some indication of which direction to go. I'm driving blind. I expand my search as far as Bangor and back again.

On the return leg, I think to myself, that was probably the wrong move, they would've been more likely to travel into Belfast, or at least around it.

In a maze of familiar roads, I finally find myself lost.

I start to find it hard to see as I rub my tearing eyes with the sleeve of my jumper, which I also use to wipe my nose when I lose all control over my emotions.

My driving becomes more erratic, accelerating hard around corners and out of junctions. Topping it out at over a hundred miles per hour in a fifty zone on the dual carriageway. The fuel light comes on and I slow to a stop at the side of the road. I sink over the steering wheel and then throw myself back in my seat in anger. I bang the back of my head against the headrest repeatedly, smashing the steering wheel with my fists until my rage subsides and I'm just left with the feeling of loss.

The search ends in turning up nothing so I bite the bullet and go back to the house, admitting defeat.

I get back to find that the front door is still ajar. I get out of the car and walk up the path and into the hall of the house. Lisa has her bags packed and resting in the hall.

'Lisa, where are you?' I call.

'I'm in the living room,' she calls back weakly.

She is sat beside the house phone which is on top of the small table beside the sofa, facing the television.

'What's all that?' I ask, pointing to the hall.

'I can't stay here. How am I meant to feel safe now?'

She's right. The house isn't exactly somewhere I could call safe after what's just happened.

'They told me, when they took Layla, to wait for the call,' she explains.

'Who were they?'

'I don't know, maybe you can tell me....Michael.'

'Lisa...,' I reach out to comfort her but she slaps my hand away violently.

'Who are they? I don't know what the fuck is going on here, help me, please. Why do they think someone called Michael lives here?'

I take a second, I can't do that much more damage.

'I used to be involved, down in Dublin. I got caught doing a drug run back up over the border. The cops picked me up with a hundred grand worth of cocaine.

'What? I don't get it, what do you mean you were involved? Like a gang?'

'Yeah, like a gang.'

'But, I thought you grew up in Belfast? Or is that a lie?'

'No, I did grow up here. I moved to Dublin when I was twenty. My mum and dad kicked me out because of the trouble I kept bringing home. When I got caught by the

10

cops they offered me a deal. No jail time and protective custody for the names and other sensitive information on the gang.'

'So, you're a rat?' Lisa asks.

'Yeah, I got a new name, a new house, that's when I met you.'

'Michael? That's you're real name?'

'Michael O'Connell,' I admit.

'I'm married to a criminal,' she mutters, putting a hand against her forehead.

'I turned my life around. I went straight. That's when I met you.'

'I don't even know you, do I?'

'You do, you've always known the real me, I didn't fake that.'

'Really? You could never trust me enough to tell me this before?'

'I didn't want you to worry or ruin what we have.'

'I haven't even rung the cops yet,' Lisa gets to her feet but I grab her arm, stopping her.

'You can't call the cops or we won't get Layla back.'

'David, I have to. I mean, Michael. God, what am I even saying?'

'I'll get her back but you need to trust me.'

She shrugs my grip off. 'Get off me. You stay away from me!'

She gets up and walks out, our eyes avert each other as she passes. I hear her pick up her bags followed swiftly by the slamming of the front door.

I take a seat on the sofa in the dark beside the phone.

I remain there for hours on end, not even getting up to eat or drink. I don't switch the television on to distract myself or even close the curtains to turn on the lights. I sit

11

in the darkness with my thoughts of what will happen from here.

Where is Layla, is she okay and what do they want?

I constantly check my phone for any calls or even texts.

I don't get anything, not even from Lisa. I leave it alone for a couple of hours before looking again at half eleven.

I lay down and try to get comfortable on the sofa, emotionally drained. That's when the call comes.

The house phone starts to ring.

I spring up and answer as swiftly as I can.

'Hello?'

'Have I got your attention now Michael?'

I recognise the voice straight away, even after all of these years. I know it's Tommy, my old boss, the head of the gang.

'You've got it, now what do you want?' I reply sternly and calmly.

'What happened to the drop?'

'The cops got it.'

'Bullshit, you traded it as evidence didn't you? Alongside the names for witness protection.'

'I didn't need the drugs for that, I just needed the names.'

'Look how far that got you. New name, new city, wife and kids now too eh?'

'Just leave my family out of this OK?'

'Listen, I don't give a single fuck what happened to the drugs, all I care about is that you pay back what you owe.'

'Tommy, I don't have that kind of money lying around. We're renting this house.'

'Well, it looks like you need to pull a plan right and quick then doesn't it?'

12

'C'mon, you've gotta give me some time here, you know that.'

'You're right Michael, you're right. You have five days.'

'Tommy, where the fuck am I gonna raise a hundred grand in five days?'

'That's your problem, not mine.'

'Is Layla OK?'

'She's fine. We haven't touched a hair on her head.'

'Let me talk to her.'

'Not gonna happen.'

'I need to know she's all right, otherwise, you get nothing.'

'Fine, what do you wanna know?'

'Is she all right and….the song I used to sing to her every night to get her off to sleep.'

'I'll get back to you on that one. Chat again soon.'

The line goes dead.

Time to get to work I think.

I close the blinds, switch on the lights and go to the kitchen. I grab the bottle of whiskey stashed in the cupboard under the sink and grab a glass from another. I also take a bowl from the sink and take it all into the living room. I place them all on the glass coffee table. I pour myself a glass of whiskey.

I go to my coat hanging over the sofa arm and take out a packet of cigarettes, I light one up and start to use the bowl as my ashtray. I start to rack my brain for ideas of how to raise the money. The immediate thoughts jump to getting a loan or committing a robbery. It is a serious amount of money to get. Whatever way I end up doing it, I know it won't be easy.

13

A past I once knew, one I thought I left behind, has finally come back to haunt me.

Murphy's Law.

***

My eyes have gotten heavy. It's been nearly an hour since I spoke to Tommy. Is he going to even call back?

I start to lose the hope of a phone call and my body starts to give in to sleep. I blink my eyes, trying to wake myself up, defiant against sleep.

The phone starts to ring.

When I pick it up, I hear Tommy mockingly recite Layla's favourite song.

Tommy hangs up and the line goes dead.

The words sing in my head like a haunting prayer for the rest of the night until I finally succumb to sleep.

DAY ONE

I wake up just a couple of hours later, unable to get back to sleep.

I spend my time staring into the darkness, waiting for the sunlight to pierce the room to kick start the new day. The adrenaline is still fresh when I go off to get a quick shower and a change of clothes. I have to bump up my appearance for the bank. I've decided that I have to lift all of my savings and try my luck to see if they will give me any sort of loan. Anything will help towards reaching my target amount.

I put on my best suit after the shower.
A light grey suit with a blue tie.
I used it for a friend's wedding two years ago.
I haven't used it since. It fits just the same.
I polish my black shoes before I put them on, finally fixing my hair with some hair wax. I look at the mirror to see myself smartly dressed with an aura of professionalism. I get my legal documents from the kitchen cupboard for the bank; my driver's licence, a bank statement and a crunched up household bill.

I get into the car and make my way into Belfast. I get a space in the underground car park in Victoria Square. It's

15

always an overly expensive place to park. I think it might cost less to just accept a ticket.

I walk to my bank which is just off Donegal Square. I used to always find banks intimidating, buildings full of wealthy people, always smartly dressed and well-spoken.

I always felt like a bum when I used to go in and have a sit down with one of the clerks about service on my account. But today, I feel like I at least seem that I belong here, that I am on their level because of my suit and unshakable confidence because, if they turned me down for a loan, I'm not any worse off.

I go in bulletproof, I've nothing of value to lose.

I have a rucksack with me as I plan to lift any amount I can in cash.

In the end, I'm declined a loan or any type of credit. I resort to doing the only thing left to do, empty my accounts. I empty my savings account as well as another savings account I had set up for Layla after she was born.

I walk away from the desk with just under six grand, all in bundled notes in my rucksack.

I head towards the exit of the bank to make my way back to the busy shops of Victoria Square, but on the way, I hear my name being called. 'Michael!' I hear someone shout. I have an initial sense of panic as I hear my real name being called. I turn around to find a balding man in dirty overalls leaving the queue and walking towards me.

His name is Andy, we grew up on the same council estate as kids and played a lot of football together. Nowadays, he works as a mechanic. He's my mechanic. If anything goes wrong with the car, he is my go-to guy. He's a perfect example of why I chose to live just outside of

Belfast with Lisa, no one would recognise me there. I've had some near misses when we came into the city centre but the thing is, most of my old friends and people I once knew have all grown up, moved on or simply forgot about me, which is probably for the best but also bitter-sweet.

'Hey, Andy, how ya been?' I ask.

'Flat out mate, working on two at the minute. Got a text late last night from a guy with a mangled Audi. In here to settle some debts and straight back to the garage. You in to do some shopping today?'

'Nah, just stupid bank stuff that needed sorting.'

'Ah fair enough, here, do you know Carl is home?'

'Is he? I didn't even know. I haven't heard from him.'

'Yeah, he was in the other day with a banged-up Clio that needed a new radiator.'

'Ah right. Still skint then?'

'Ha, yeah, that's the thing. If you're talking to him could you tell him I need the other hundred by the end of the week?'

'Yeah, no problem.'

'Cheers, gotta run. See you later,' he says as he starts backing away and rushing back to the queue.

I leave the bank and make my way back to the busy shops of Victoria Square.

I take the escalator down to the car park and get back into the car.

I throw the rucksack onto the passenger seat and put the keys into the ignition. I hesitate, looking back at the rucksack, thinking.

Inside that bag is six thousand pounds of the ransom, nowhere near the asking price. Everything that I have doesn't even make a dent in what I need.

17

Maybe it's time to invest.

I start up the car and leave the underground.

I cruise around aimlessly, buying myself time, time to think before I choose my destination.

I decide to just drive home and regroup after circling the city centre twice over.

On the way back, a road closure on the motorway forces me to take the long way home. On the way, all that enters my mind is the question, is Carl really back? I pass his flat this way, should I stop in? Things have been damaged between us since I left at eighteen. He went on to join the army so he's rarely home. The last time we last saw each other was at dad's funeral.

I come upon the council estate of Tullycarnet.

It's always distinguishable by the massive loyalist murals painted onto the walls of the flats facing the road.

I turn down into the road that takes me to the front of the flats. I let the engine run when I pull up to the curb and spy Carl's car parked a little further up the road. It must be his because it's the only Clio around here.

I look up to the top window of the first tower block of flats. It's been Carl's home since he was seventeen. He moved in just a year before I left for Dublin.

I could use his help to figure all of this out, but then, would he?

Does he still resent me for everything I put the family through?

No, I can't stand to tell him that I'm responsible for his niece's kidnapping. This is all my doing, my problem.

I'll figure it out like I always have.

18

***

It's just after two o'clock when I get home to the empty house.

The silence seems to echo, as well as the constant feeling that I shouldn't be here, that I'm wasting time.

I go to my bedroom and take a seat on the cold, wrecked bed.

What next? I think to myself.

I think about the rucksack of cash that I've left in the hall. My plan of investment is risky but I deem it is necessary under the circumstances.

I go over to the bookcase by the door and pluck out a small notepad. Skipping to the back of the notepad until I reach the last page.

There I find a handwritten phone number with a name beside it. Colin, he used to be like a brother to me. We both left for Dublin together to join with a crew down there. When the whole thing went down, he's the one person I didn't give up but he let the others believe different of course. He still runs with the same crowd as far as I know.

The only reason I think he might help is because he has owed me a few favours over the years that I never cashed in on.

I enter the number into my phone and call it.

A defensive voice answers.

'Who is this?'

'Colin, you alone?'

'Who is this? How did you get this number?'

'It's Michael.'

'Michael? Fuck sake, I shouldn't be talking to you.'

'I need your help mate,' I say.

'Look, I appreciate you needed a way out, I'm grateful you didn't give my name in but, I cannot be talking to you, you know that. Do you know how many guys you put away with what you told the cops? Wallace is serving eight years.'

'I did what I had to. You know how things had been in the build-up to the run. I never wanted to do it. I wanted to get out months before that.'

'Yeah but, you do your time like a man and keep your mouth shut.'

'Did you know they threatened my family?'

Colin stays silent for a moment, I know that they probably left that part out when he heard about what had happened.

'Yeah Colin, they threatened to hurt my family if I didn't go through with it. My mum and dad. That's how the crew had started to treat me. I wasn't one of their brothers any more, I was the lackey,' I tell him.

'They think you took the drop for yourself. That's why they are coming after you for the hundred grand. They think you stashed it somewhere before you talked to the cops,' Colin explains.

'I know, I know. Look, I'm not trying to land you in shit, I just need a quick favour.'

'I don't know. No promises but what do you need?'

'Do you have any pieces lying around?'

The line goes quiet for a moment.

'Michael, you're smart. Don't try and start a war. Take this to the cops.'

'If I go to the cops Tommy will kill her. We both know the man he is.'

'What are you gonna do?'

'I'm going to get the money,' I say without hesitation.

'How long did he give you?'

'Five days.'

'Christ, where are you gonna get a hundred grand in five days?'

'I don't know yet but I have to. I've no other choice. If I go to the cops, I'll never see her again. They will leave her in an unmarked grave if they think the heat is coming down on them.'

'Well, I know a guy up that way that could maybe help you out.'

'Can you set up a meet?' I ask.

'Sure, when?'

'Tonight?'

'Tonight? Fuck sake, Michael. Could you maybe give me a bit more time than that?'

'It has to be tonight.'

'Right, OK, OK, I'll give my guy a call now and see what he can do.'

'Thanks.'

'Yeah sure, I'll ring you back in ten minutes.'

The call ends and I lay back on the bed looking at the ceiling, wishing the time away. I start to drift off when the phone vibrates.

I answer.

'Hello?'

'He can meet you at nine tonight but no later. You have to be there on time.'

'OK, where's he at?'

'There's a caravan site, just outside of Newcastle. If you go down there, his caravan is painted red with the Manchester football club badge on the side.'

'This guy straight?' I ask.

'Yeah, he's straight. You won't get any trouble from him or his guys as long as you don't piss on their doorstep.'

'Thanks, Colin.'

'I think that's us even. Just don't tell anyone we were talking.'

'Your name won't come up.'

'Good luck mate,' he says before the line goes dead.

***

I spend the afternoon mostly smoking cigarettes and downing countless cups of coffee, I'm an addict for the stuff. It nears seven o'clock so I grab my car keys and leave the house in the dying sun.

I drive around the outside of Belfast and then onward towards the county roads of County Down. The road falls into the darkness the whole way apart from the brief breaks of light from the small towns and petrol stations.

The white lines of the road are my only constant companion and they guide me until I finally see the towering black masses in the skyline that are the Mourne Mountains.

I start to slow down as I come up on the first lights of the town of Newcastle. It is a seaside town at the foot of the Mourne Mountains. It's a popular summer destination too, especially for people from Belfast.

I see the caravan park up ahead on the left. I turn into it, everything is dark and quiet. It has quite an eerie feeling to it. I use my headlights as searchlights, looking for the caravan in red. All of the caravans are tucked closely together and things such as bedsheets and clothing hang on the lines tied between them, obscuring the view even further.

As I get to the far end of the land, I see the distinctive red caravan.

It is one of the older models of the lot. I park in a space beside it and turn the engine off. I take a look around before stepping out.

I can't help but feel on edge, especially because of the reason that I am here. Then I start to second guess everything.

What if Colin is setting me up?

Does he really still have my back after all of this time or is he playing me?

I finally realise that I am being paranoid and I reason with myself. The cold air sends shivers down my body as I step out into it. Everything is dead silent. The red caravan is vacant of light but I walk up to the door and knock anyway. This is the agreed time after all.

I hear a few knocks and thuds come from inside. A light comes on and the door opens.

Stood on the inside is a large, balding man in a badly stained white t-shirt and black tracksuit bottoms.

'You Colin's guy?' he asks.

'Yeah.'

He leans out of the doorway, he almost head-butts me but I lean back in time.

He looks around the darkness for any sign of life.

'Alright, get in,' he grumbles.

23

I step inside and he closes the door behind me.

The inside of the caravan is a complete mess. The floor is full of crumbs and odd bits and ends. The wooden décor of the kitchen is worn, scratched and dented and the small dining seat area is covered in clothes.

'Over here,' he beckons, guiding me to the sofa lining the back window of the caravan. He puts his large hands underneath the cushions and lifts them up to reveal a compartment in the wooden base of the sofa.

It's too dark to see inside but just as the man pushes the rest of the cushions out of the way, he then reaches in and pulls out a black bin bag. It makes loud and heavy metallic clunking noises as he lifts it into the air. He brings it over to the dining area.

He uses one arm to drag the clothes off the table and onto the floor whilst lifting the bag onto the cleared table with the other.

He opens the mouth of the bag and puts his hand inside.

'So, what will it be?' he asks in a serious tone.

He pulls out a small black handgun from the bag.

'Your standard 9mm, decent clip size. If you've ever watched any American cop film, you're bound to have seen one of these.'

He continues to empty more handguns from the bag and onto the table.

'Any of these take your fancy?' he asks.
I study the guns. There are a couple of small revolvers but I score them out right away. They've only five-shot guns and would take forever to reload, especially in the heat of a firefight.

I choose the two that look to be in the best condition. The 9mm and a Glock.

'I'll take them two,' I say, pointing them out.

24

'That'll set you back five hundred, pal,' he says as he goes to one of the kitchen cupboards and opens it.

I look around. This can't be it, a couple of handguns?

He comes back from the cupboard with several small boxes in his arms. He drops them on to the table.

'Bullets. Guessing you'll be needing a couple of boxes.'

'This all of your stock?' I ask.

He stops dead. 'What do you mean?' he replies in a slightly suspicious voice.

'I was hoping you'd have something more...heavy duty.'

'Right,' he says, sizing me up with his eyes. 'You got the cash for that kind of kit?'

'I've six grand in cash.'

His eyes widen and he fights to keep a grin from appearing across his red, frowning face. 'So, that's a yes. Follow me.'

He goes to the door and picks a coat up from the floor next to it. He wriggles his hands inside the pockets once he puts it on until he hears the jingle of keys. 'C'mon,' he ushers as he opens the door.

I leave the guns and ammo on the table and follow him outside.

The cold hits me again and I bring up the collar of my coat to protect as much of my face as possible.

I follow the man around the back of the caravan.

This is the end of the caravan park, beyond lays a field that disappears into the cold, dark night.

The orange lights of a Range Rover flash and the sound of the locks opening echo. I didn't see the Rover as we came around as it is black and blends perfectly into its surroundings.

25

I follow the man to the rear of the Rover and he opens up the boot. White interior lights shine onto a blanket. The man carefully reaches in and folds it back to reveal a small collection of rifles.

'Harder to get these ones. Pick your poison. They're all lethal wee numbers.'

I make a quick selection of two automatic rifles and lift them out.

'Fuck, straight in, no messing about from you eh?' he says.

'I'll need mags for these too,' I demand.

'OK, all in all, that's gonna set you back three grand, let's get these inside until we sort out the money. There are clips for these inside too. Think I have around seven for each.'

Three grand, that's half of my money.

Right now, I don't know what else to spend the cash on, or anything better to spend it on. We go back inside the caravan, I grab my rucksack on passing the car and it's all counted inside. He bags up everything for me and I make my exit swiftly.

I leave the caravan park and start the long drive home. The roads are quieter than they had been coming here and the fog has settled on certain parts of the countryside. It would come at me on the long straights, my headlights illuminating it, making it look more like thick clouds of smoke as it skips over the bonnet and slides over the windscreen.

A light startles me from inside the car. I find its source coming from the passenger seat, it's my phone. I pick it up to see Lisa is calling me, I answer.

'Lisa?'

'David, I mean, Michael...whatever you wanna be called. I'm just calling to let you know that I'm just off the phone to the police. They're starting to look for Layla.'

'What? Lisa, what the fuck are you doing? I told you don't call them.'

'Then what? Then what? We sit back and hope for the best?'

'I told you, I will fix this.'

'Fuck you, David, you caused this. It's your fault Layla is out there somewhere, crying on her own without her mummy and daddy, scared senseless.'

I tighten my squeeze on the steering wheel, releasing just some of my rage that's building.

'What did you tell them?' I ask.

'I told them everything. Even what you told me. They want to talk to you, I think you should go see them.'

'You didn't Lisa.'

'They said they will bring you in for questioning.'

'You don't know what you've done, you stupid bitch!'

'Go fuck yourself, David, I want a divorce.'

She hangs up.

I start shouting until my throat hurts, bashing the steering wheel and dashboard, causing the car to even sway off course in between the strikes.

When I do get my anger under check, I focus it into putting the accelerator down and racing back to the house before the cops get there.

When I get there, I run from the car.

I bash right into the front door, quicker than I can push down the handle but it remains solid. I try the handle again, forgetting it's locked. I scramble for the key in my coat pocket and open the door. I stomp into the living room.

The thing that catches my eye is a photo frame rested on top of the mantelpiece of the fireplace. It is a white frame. Inside it is a photograph of me, Lisa and Layla from last year. A cold numbness strikes me all of a sudden. I close my eyes, standing in the dark on my own, without the family I once had. When I open my eyes, I look down to my hands which are visibly shaking.

I take the photo frame and throw it against the wall with all of my strength. I run to the television and kick it off its stand. I rip the cushions off the sofas and throw them in every direction. The cold numbness has been replaced with a burning hot rush, a pain in the pit of my stomach with tears streaming from my eyes.

I dash up the stairs, stumbling and almost falling on my way up. The upstairs hallway is in complete darkness, only the moonlight from my bedroom pierces the hallway. On my way towards the bedroom, I see a door ajar on my right, it's Layla's room. My heart slows and calms, I walk slowly towards it and gently push the door open.

Her room is the same mess she leaves it in every day. I go over to her bed where she has put a teddy bear beside her pillow close to the wall. I pick it up and look at it, imagining her cuddling it, imagining it watching over her.

I remember this teddy. I got this one for her.

I won it at an arcade in Portrush last summer when Lisa and I went away for the weekend to celebrate our anniversary. I must've spent twelve pounds to win it but it's probably only worth half of that. I put it against my cheek, a desperate attempt to connect with Layla.

I take it away from my face and put it back on the bed.

I put it into bed as I would with Layla, tucking it in under the covers and positioning it just right with the pillow.

I leave the room and close the door silently behind me before going to my bedroom.

I reach for the bedroom light but I stop. It might be best to keep the house in darkness.

If the cops show up, I don't want to give my position away from the start. At least this way, the house seems empty, unless anyone has called in the noise I made downstairs. I open the large wardrobe and grab a large rucksack from the bottom of it.

I start to pack my clothes frantically into it. As I zip the bag shut, I hear the front door open and slam close again. I carefully edge towards the window. Looking out, I see no signs of the cops or any new cars parked outside.

I hear more noises from downstairs.

I focus on the bedroom door and beyond into the darkness of the hall.

I carefully sneak towards the hall, trying not to make any sounds with my footsteps. I look over the bannister, down the stairs. Everything is quiet and still.

I creep my way down the stairs, checking all around with every step. On the final step, someone tackles me into the wall at the foot of the stairs. We struggle, trying to out wrestle each other. In the midst of the struggle that travels from the stairs, into the hall, we bounce off the walls, knocking pictures down. We throw punches at each other but we never fully escape each other's grip.

I eventually manage to slip out of his grip. It's too dark to make out the finer details of his face. He comes at me again with a barrage of punches. I return fire.

I catch his chin with a punch and he drops to the floor. I launch on top of him on the ground to finish him off. Throwing my fists as hard as I can down on him, he manages to block them well with his arms. He grabs the back of my neck, dragging me down whilst repositioning himself to a seated position. He head-butts me and lets go of me. I stumble back, trying to get my feet underneath myself but I fall back onto my butt.

Heavy breathing breaks the silence and space between us as we both sit tired and beaten on opposite sides of the small hallway.

That's when I get the chance to properly study his face, now that my eyes have adjusted.

Andy wasn't lying, he is home.

'Carl?'

My brother doesn't look much like me. People were always surprised to learn that we were brothers. He is slightly bigger than me, with close-shaven hair. He has the more chiselled look of us both.

'Michael,' he says, catching his breath, 'you stupid bastard.'

'What are you talking about?'

'I just heard about what happened. It's all over the news, all over the radio.'

'Can we do this later? The cops are on their way here right now. I've got a car outside full of guns in the boot.'

'What are you planning to do? Get yourself killed?' Carl asks.

I get to my feet. 'I've to get a hundred grand in five days. I'm getting Layla back.'

I turn my back on Carl and go back upstairs to get my rucksack of clothes. On my way back down the stairs, Carl is nowhere to be seen, he is gone. I leave the house and go to my car.

At that moment, the car's headlights come on and the engine starts. Going to driver's door, I see Carl sat at the wheel.

'What are you doing?' I shout.

'You're gonna have a hard time doing this on your own. Now, get in.'

I want to argue with him but I can't, he's right. I do need his help.

***

We drive into Belfast and I start to wonder where Carl plans on going.

'So where are we going?' I ask him finally.

'Dad's house. I still have my key,' he says.

As we get closer to our parents' old house, I start to recount memories of my past from scenery we pass. School grounds we used to sneak into for drinking sessions, the alleyways that were hotspots for after school fights, the old row of shops which were the only ones we could get cigarettes from without being asked for I.D. Everything started pouring back at once and it feels quite overwhelming as things are so much different now. It feels like it was a different lifetime.

We finally get to our old housing estate of Cregagh, on the very edge of east Belfast.

The streets are quiet and empty but I start to feel anxious.

I haven't been back to this house since the funeral.

Me and Carl were on the verge of putting dad up in a home before he passed.

He wasn't the same after mum was gone and our uncle Harry, his brother, spent a lot of his nights going round to the house to clean up and help dad with making proper dinners instead of his usual microwavable shit. I wish I had of been there more for him, I think we both do.

I was down in Dublin, caught up in a turf war with a rival gang and Carl was on the other side of the world on his second tour of duty. Neither of us had the heart to sell the house.

We just couldn't stand giving the house away. As far as we were concerned, this was still mum and dad's house and it would kill me to see anyone taking it over. I'd rather see it knocked to the ground.

We eventually end up outside the house. It's the same as ever.

The paint has started to flake off the white garden wall. The garden has been kept nice, however. Probably thanks to uncle Harry, he must still tend to the house. Carl opens the front door to let us in. I'm surprised he has managed to keep his key for all of this time. I lost mine after the first two weeks of having it.

We switch the lights on and I go off to explore the house ahead of Carl who closes the door behind us. The living room still has the old, dated furniture. Including an old, black leather armchair that my mum tried to get rid of for years but dad was too stubborn to let it go, it was his throne. The kitchen has been updated from the brown wooden doors Carl and I used to swing on when we were younger. Now everything is contemporary furnishing.

Aluminium cupboards, marble worktops accompanied by a large American style fridge freezer that dominates a corner of the kitchen.

'Michael!' Carl calls, seemingly from the living room.

I go back to the living room where he is stood looking out of the window blinds.

He turns as he hears me enter the room.

'So what's the plan?' he asks.

'To be honest, I don't know yet. I've got bits and pieces but….not the full picture yet,' I admit.

He lets out a great sigh and sits on the end of the sofa. I take a seat on the other end of it.

'What happened?' Carl asks.

'Did a run. It was meant for Coleraine but I got pulled, just over the border.'

'What were you carrying?'

'A hundred grand of coke.'

'Fuck me,' Carl exclaims, rubbing his hand over his head.

'Yeah,' I say, holding my head in my hands and looking at the floor.

'They offered me a deal,' I continue. 'They'd let me walk and put me into protective custody if I gave up everyone down in Dublin.'

'And you took it?' Carl asks.

'Of course. No matter what I did from that point on, I would have a target on my forehead anyway. I just lost an entire shipment that we couldn't afford to lose and if I took the noble route of going to jail, Tommy would've had me whacked on the inside. So really, it was a lose-lose situation.'

'Did you not talk to your wife first? Lisa?' Carl asks.

'I didn't meet Lisa until a year later. She didn't know anything about that side of me until last night.'

A silence falls between us.

I start to think about how me and Lisa met. She worked in the petrol station at the time, quite close to where we live now. I'd always stop there to fill up.

Most times that I stopped there she was working. She always caught my eye, always smiling, there was something sweet and honest about her. She was like the kind of girl that you'd have a crush on in school but were always too shy to talk to. We talked every time though, the chemistry was instant.

Sometimes I'd hold up the queue talking to her.

'So how long do we have?' Carl asks.

'Five days, well four now.'

'What are our options?'

'I don't even know where they are, where they are keeping Layla.'

'You've got a car full of guns, don't you? If these fuckers want a war, let's give them one.'

'I was thinking the exact same thing when I went and got them. But it's a sure-fire way to get us all killed.'

'What do you want to do then?' Carl asks.

'I don't know, I'll come up with something.'

'Well, I'm going to bed,' Carl says, standing up. 'I'll make a couple of calls and see what I can work out.'

'Who to?' I ask.

'I'll tell you tomorrow if anything comes up.' I hear him stop at the door. 'Maybe the only way out of this mess is the same way you got into it,' he says before disappearing into the hall.

DAY TWO

I wake up with immense pain in my shoulder. I take my weight off it and roll onto my back on the sofa, kicking off my coat that becomes entangled in my legs at the bottom. The living room door swings in and hits the arm of the sofa. Carl storms in.

'C'mon get up!' he shouts.

I get off the sofa and pick my shoes up off the floor. Sitting back to put them back on, I look up to see Carl coming towards me, throwing my coat on the sofa beside me.

'What is it?' I ask.

'We've got a meet to get to.'

'Who with?'

'A guy I know. He might be able to help us out, now c'mon,' he commands as he throws on his coat.

I get my shoes and coat on and rush out the door behind Carl.

We get in the car and he starts driving.

We get onto the motorway and drive to the west side of Belfast.

I used to have friends from here as a kid so I know the streets vaguely from my childhood drinking stage.

We enter one of the housing estates. It has small modest houses like those where our parent's house is. But it is not them that we stop at, instead, it is a small run-down bar that we stop at.

'This is it,' Carl says as he opens the car door and gets out.

I follow Carl inside and up to the bar where a young girl has her phone laid flat on the bar, texting.

'Hello,' Carl greets her.

She continues to play on her phone. 'Hey,' she says in an unconcerned voice.

'Where's Willy?' Carl asks.

The girl's attention then diverts from her phone for the first time as her eyes draw up to meet Carl's.

'He's out the back,' she says.

Carl walks around the bar and to a door behind the girl.

'Hey! You're not allowed back there!' she shouts after him.

He continues through the door, after a second, I follow.

The young girl is powerless to stop us.

I make my way through to the back of the building, boxes upon boxes are stacked ceiling-high against the walls. I push my way past some empty storage trolleys and go to the fire door that is slightly ajar, letting in a slither of daylight.

I come outside into an alley, I look down to my right where I see Carl stood facing a man leaning against the wall with a cigarette. I go to them and slowly their conversation comes into earshot.

'I don't know if he'll do you that much. Who's this?' the man says pointing to me approaching them.

'This is my brother Michael, Michael this is Willy.'

'How's it going?' I greet.

'So how much could he do?' Carl continues his conversation with Willy.

'I'll need to speak to him first. I mean, if we were talking pills, I could definitely sort you guys out,' Willy says as he stubs out his cigarette.

'Nah, we're not interested in pills. Anyone can shift that shit and not come out pennies up. Strictly coke mate.'

'Alright, OK. I'll talk to my guy and give you a call.'

'Alright, thanks.'

'But one thing Carl, not trying to say anything bad about you here. I've never had any problems with you, you're a stand-up guy but just don't fuck me about,' Willy's tone changing from laid back to serious.

'Fair enough,' Carl replies.

Willy reaches out and pats Carl on the shoulder. 'Cause if you do, I won't be the one facing the consequences.'

Willy goes back into the bar through the fire door.

'What the fuck's that about?' I ask Carl.

Carl starts walking down the alley, I walk quickly to catch up.

'What was that all about?' I ask again.

'A deal,' Carl explains.

'What deal? A fucking coke deal?'

'Yep, a hundred grands worth.'

'What? Did I hear you right? What the fuck you paying that with? Hopes and dreams?'

Carl stops.

'Listen, how else are we gonna get Layla back? We're outta options. Unless you plan on robbing a bank, this is the only way. You have to understand, the thing that got you into this mess might be the only thing that can get you out of it!' Carl snaps.

We don't talk the rest of the way back to the car, Even the car ride is an awkward silence, broken only by the songs on the radio. Then a news report comes on that catches our attention.

"Police are looking for the father of missing girl, Layla Isaac. Mr Isaac has not been seen since his daughter's disappearance and police have not ruled him as a suspect in their inquiries."

I look to Carl who looks back at me from the wheel.

'Well that's not much of a surprise is it?' he asks.

'Not really, just adds to the shit storm,' I say, leaning my head back on the headrest.

We spend the rest of the day driving around, visiting various people or contacts we both have, or at least used to have. Carl tries to arrange more deals but no one seems to be biting. I try calling on my closest friends for a lend of money but altogether, they can only give me a thousand. Extremely generous on short notice but not a game-changer.

Thankfully I managed to avoid questions about Layla. Word must have not spread that much yet, I'm glad.

I'm ashamed to admit it, but Carl might actually be right. Unless we plan on robbing a bank, like he said the only way we could pull this off is the potential deal with his contact, Willy.

It starts to get dark when we decide to head back to our parents' house.

'I have to make a stop on the way back. Need to get some food for the house,' Carl says.

We stop at a supermarket overlooking the carriageway at Newtownbreda.

'You coming in or you wanna wait in the car?' Carl asks after we find a parking space.

'Might as well come in,' I take off my seatbelt and go over to the store with Carl.

We enter the store and Carl stops in front of the stall by the doors.

'Here,' he hands me some cash. 'Get some milk, ham, that sort of shit. I need to grab some cigs here.'

I take the cash and walk deeper into the store. I stroll around, taking my time. I go on a detour and check out the latest DVDs that are on sale. Hardly any new releases and the ones that are half decent are way overpriced. Who pays twenty pounds for a DVD nowadays? You have all of them digital online stores where you can get them for around four pounds. It won't be long until these shelves are empty and everything becomes digitized.

I scan the cool aisles for milk. Once I do find it, I think I must've passed this aisle at least twice in my search.

I feel my phone vibrating, is it Lisa? Maybe I should really get rid of this. The only reason I keep it is for the outlandish chance that somehow, Layla finds a way to charge her phone or get another to call me back on. I lift my phone out of my pocket to see it is Carl that is calling. Probably with more to add to the shopping list.

'Hey, what is it?'

'Cops are here. They came to the same counter as me. One of them was buying some of that e-cig liquid crap. Then this old woman came up to them. Said she recognised you and you were in here. They're splitting up and looking for you, there's two of em, you've gotta move.'

'Shit, right OK.'

I hang up, drop the milk on the floor and start running to the far end of the store. I try to stay close to the aisles, checking my back to see if I can see any of them.

I see a pair of black boots stepping out at the end of the aisles. I dash into the next closest aisle and start to rush up it, keeping my eyes forward, hoping, praying that the other doesn't head me off. I get to the end and peer out from beside the bread stack.

The clothing section is adjacent to where I am. More cover and more places to hide. I risk it and sprint over, keeping low. I hide behind one of the racks and look out. I can't see any of them. I move slowly, deeper into the clothing section. How am I going to get out? Should I try the front door? Will they have it covered? What about the fire escapes?

My phone starts to buzz. I pop up to a standing position, looking over the racks for any movement before kneeling down and taking the call.

It's Carl again.

'Hey.'

'Hey where are you?' he asks.

'I'm at the clothes section.'

'OK, go! They're down the far end beside the drinks.'

I get up and start hurrying towards the tills.

'Is the front door clear?' I ask, running with the phone to my ear.

'Use the fire escape, there's a few people near the door. You don't wanna be seen.'

'Where is the fire escape?' I ask as I leave the clothes section and come out in front of the tills, searching for the fire escape.

'It's behind the tills, beside the café bit.'

I try my best to act casual as there is a woman on one of the tills near me. I pocket my phone and walk through one of the tills and make my way towards the café, all the time double-checking all around for a surprise appearance from the fuzz.

I start to slow as I spot the fire door.

I get right up next to it, my hand resting on the panic bar. I give one last check around. The few shoppers and store staff scattered around aren't looking.

I push open the door and spill out into the night, bursting into a sprint once I am on the other side.

I hear the faint slam of the door in the distance behind me as I am already near the front entrance of the store again. I divert my path, scared of being spotted. I jump up into the shrubbery that surrounds the car park. I push past the leaves and branches as I circle the car park, trying to get as close to the car as possible.

Why did we have to park in the centre of the car park?

My clothes become entangled and I feel loose branches plucking at my jeans as I get further around the shrubbery.

I take a knee and try calling Carl but he doesn't answer after three continuous attempts. I can't stay here, I can't risk Carl leaving without me either.

We are still a good distance from home.

I make my way out of the shrubbery and jump down from the small wall, down into the car park. I use the parked cars as cover and go from one to the other until I get to our car. I check the passenger door - it opens.

'For fuck's sake Carl, you still don't know how to lock the fucking door,' I mutter before I climb inside.

He never locked car doors. To him, he never saw the sense in it. People couldn't steal the car if you've got the keys, that was his take on it.

One time, our dad asked him to get his wallet from the car, Carl forgot to lock it afterwards and someone stole our brand new curtains from the back seat. What kind of sick fucks steal curtains?

I close the door once I'm inside the car and hide on the floor in the back. I spend the time looking at the ceiling of the car. Every white flash of passing headlights gives me a fright and every voice that passes the car makes me hold my breath as if it were loud enough to give me away.

After what must've been ten minutes - which felt like an hour - the boot of the car opens and I hear the rustle of plastic bags being placed inside.

The driver's door opens and Carl climbs in.

'What took you so long?' I whisper in an aggravated tone.

Carl jumps in his seat, startled by my presence. 'Fucking hell, you scared the shit outta me!'

I manoeuvre to sit up but Carl stretches his hand out into the back.

'No, no stay down, the cops are still hanging around,' Carl says.

'What were you doing?'

'Getting the stuff. Got a few drinks too, think we've earned it.'

'Ah right, so I'm getting hunted by the cops but you go ahead with your shopping list?'

'Might as well, already here aren't we? I saw you go out the fire escape so I knew you were home and dry.'

'Oh that's another thing,' I say.

'What's that?'

'Can you start locking my fucking car?'

'Shut the fuck up or I'll hit the speed bumps at forty on the way back. Now lay down and shut up.'

Carl starts up the engine and I feel the car start to move. I see the flashes of red and blue lights as we leave the car park.

Once we get back to our parents' house, I help Carl in with the bags.

I put all of the bags on the kitchen counter and leave them for Carl to sort out. I take out one of the beers and knock the cap off using the edge of the marble worktop on my way out the back door to the garden.

I go over and take a seat on the small wall beside the grass and fix my gaze in wonder at the large tree at the bottom of the garden. Slugging my beer down, I remember how the tree used to always play a vital part in my childhood games here. It used to have magical powers, it even had a face, a face only I could make out from the patterns in the bark.

There was one time when me and Johnny Peters skipped school and climbed it out of boredom. He could only reach the second large branch. I wanted to prove that I could reach the top, half because I could, the other part of me wanted to see the view from up there. Maybe I could even see over the top of the house. I spent six hours stuck in that tree. Johnny ran off cause he didn't want to get caught skipping school.

Apparently, his dad was a really tough bastard who would beat him about the house if he did something wrong.

I stayed stuck in the tree until mum and dad got back from work. My dad got so angry, I'd never seen his face so red. He always did a thing with his tongue when he was angry. He would stick out his tongue, curling it up over his upper lip whilst biting down on it. It was a sign that he was really angry.

I hear the back door open behind me.

'You coming in? You'll never guess what I've found,' Carl says in an excited voice.

'What is it?' I ask.

'Just come see,' he says as he goes back inside.

I down the last drops of my beer and go back inside.

When I come back into the kitchen I see that Carl has only put away half of the bags.

'Thought you were gonna sort these bags out?' I shout, loud enough for him to hear me wherever he might be in the house.

'I'll do it later! The stuff that needed to be put away into the fridge and the freezer is done!' he shouts back, seemingly from the living room.

The living room is in darkness, only the television screen gives light to the room. Then it's what's on the television that grasps my attention. An old, fighting video game me and Carl played almost religiously as kids.

'No fucking way!' I shout, a smile from nostalgia coming across my face.

'Hell fucking yes!' he shouts back with a chuffed voice.

He is sat on the floor, leaning his back against the sofa with a console controller in his hands. He reaches for something by his side. He throws a second controller up onto the sofa.

I open a beer with my teeth and hand it to him. I then open myself another beer, taking a sip before placing it on the floor and taking up my controller and sitting on the sofa.

'So who you gonna be?' I ask Carl as he chooses a game character to fight me with.

'Get over here!' he says in a voice mimicking the characters.

'You're always fucking him.'

'That's why I always win,' he says smugly, taking a drink of his beer as I choose my character.

We play the game over and over again.

We even start reciting old movie quotes from old favourites.

'Hey, remember this one?' Carl asks.

He puts on his best mocking voice, 'Try up the road, you get yourself a double cheese and fries for two ninety-nine!'

'I like the tuna here,' I reply in my best mocking voice.

'Bullshit asshole, no one likes the tuna here!'

'Yeah, well I do.'

'Ha, great film,' Carl says.

'We got any more beers?' I ask.

Carl looks around, empty bottles lay scattered all around us.

'I doubt we've gone through a twenty crate,' he says.

He gets up to look around as I continue to play the game. I hear him sliding the beer box across the floor towards where we are sitting.

'Seven left,' he says as he falls onto the sofa beside me, opening another one.

We sit fixed on the television screen before a blinding light comes from the floor; Carl's phone.

He nearly drops his beer as he frantically scrambles to get to it. I do my part in muting the television just before he answers the call.

'Hello? Yeah,' Carl answers.

I wait patiently as there is a long pause.

I start to try my best to guess as to what is being said from Carl's expressions.

'Yeah, that'll do. Yeah I know where it is, we won't be late. Thanks for this. Cheers mate, bye,' Carl hangs up.

'So what's happening?' I ask.

'We've got a meet tomorrow at half one. Up around Boucher Road.'

I pause for a moment in thought, something has just occurred to me.

'What is it?' Carl asks, wary of my delayed response.

'The car. The cops will be looking for my car.'

'Shit. We need to get my one from your house then. Hope the cops haven't been all over it.'

'Where did you park it? Was it on the driveway?'

'Parked it on the curb, near enough facing your house.'

'Doubt it then. People park all over the place up there,' I say.

'OK then, let's go,' Carl decides, standing up and straightening his clothes.

'Not now you nut. You've had about eight beers.'

'What if the cops spy it outside?' he asks, raising his voice.

'Then we'll move it around the corner but we aren't driving it to fucking Holywood.'

'Alright, fine then. Where're the keys?'

'In my coat,' I tell him getting up.

'Where are you going? I can get them,' he says.

'I'm coming with you to make sure you hide it properly and don't fuck it up.'

I lean over the sofa to get my coat which has fallen down the back.

'I'm not going far for fuck's sake. I'll be fine doing it myself.'

I put my coat on and take out the keys from one of the pockets. I throw them across the room at Carl who catches them.

'I don't care, my car. If I wasn't such a lightweight, I'd do it myself.'

I know Carl could always handle his drink better than me. I am starting to get blurry vision which may be a combination of both too much alcohol and a lack of sleep.

We creep out into the dead of night.

Everything is quiet. Not even a breeze to disturb the neighbour's hedge. I think sound seems to echo more on the cold nights like this one, which is why I close the front door very gently. It reminds me of old days past when I was in my late teens. Being out in the cold, amber lit streets of Belfast. At that certain stage of drunk where fatigue starts to kick in but you will yourself on to stay awake.

We quietly get into the car. Carl managed to smuggle a few beer bottles out underneath his coat. He throws them into the back seat and starts up the engine. We pull away into the night to find the perfect hiding spot. We pass through the streets of the estate, I drift off into a daydream as I look out the window. I only come back around when we reach a junction of the main road.

'Where are you going?' I ask Carl.

He pulls out on the main road.

'Carl!'

'We're already on the road so we might as well do this now.'

'No! Pull in and jump out. I'll drive us back.'

'I'm fine, look,' he says, holding his hand out straight and steady.

'I don't give a fuck, c'mon. You agreed.'

'Michael, take out your Tampon, we're fine,' he fires back as we reach about halfway up the main road.

We eventually get to my house and, to my relief, Carl gives up the steering wheel, going over to get into his own car. He starts the engine up as I turn my car around to head back down the road. I wait for him and he pulls up alongside me.

'We still need to get rid of your car,' Carl says.

'We'll burn it out somewhere,' I tell him.

'I know, follow me.'

Before I get the chance to utter a response, Carl speeds off down the street. I have a bit of a task in catching up to him. I follow him over to the retail park not far from my house. It's quite eerie at this time of night, seeing a place that is always booming with shoppers being reduced to a ghost town by night.

Carl leads me into one of the large car parks at the foot of a giant D.I.Y store. He parks his own car up, gets out and gets into mine. He reaches into the back seat and picks up another beer. He picks one out for me too but I refuse it.

'C'mon, have some fun. C'mon,' Carl says.

No matter how much I protest he won't leave it alone so I give in and take a drink.

'Might as well have some fun before we burn it eh?' Carl says.

Against my logical thinking, I let go and embrace the moment. I rev the engine loudly. Then I drop the clutch and take off, pulling up the handbrake at the end of the car park, swinging the car around in a handbrake turn before taking off again. I sway the car from side to side, throwing me and Carl side to side with it. I even try my hand at doing a doughnut but fail miserably.

'Right, OK. Let me have a go,' Carl says, slugging his beer again.

I get out of the car, finishing the last of my beer and throwing it away, hearing it smash somewhere off in the car park. I get into the passenger seat and Carl has already slid across into the driver's seat.

He has some fun with the car too, doing high-speed manoeuvres and handbrake turns. After a while, I start to get a feeling I haven't had in ages, it's travel sickness. Carl stops the car and we both agree to wrap it up and get out of here in case anyone drives past and happens to see us.

I ask how we are going to get rid of the car.

He takes off his t-shirt and asks for my lighter. After I give it to him he goes to the petrol cap and stuffs his t-shirt into it before lighting the end of it. He comes jogging back to me.

'Let's go,' he says.

'I'm driving,' I tell him.

He gets into the passenger seat and I get in and drive us out of the car park. We get to the roundabout of the retail park, I stop by the side of the road and we roll down the windows, hanging out of the car to see my car in the car park behind us.

The explosion catches us by surprise when the flames go inside the petrol tank and blows the car up. The car

49

turns into an inferno, bright enough to light up a good portion of the car park in the darkness.

I get back inside the car and start driving back to our parents' house.

Our work here is done.

DAY THREE

When I wake up, I have that dirty taste in my mouth like I hadn't brushed my teeth in weeks. My lips are dry and chapped and my head feels groggy. Despite all of this, I am comfortable here in bed, under the sheets. Everything is relaxed, the sun does its best to burst through the blinds and I hear birds singing from the open window. Then I look around to see that I am in my old bedroom in my parents' house.

Reality sinks back in that very instant. It hits me like an electric shock, like a beer fear. I get out of bed straight away, I don't have time to rest, we've got work to do.

I go straight to Carl's old room but he's not there. I find him on the sofa downstairs, his ass falling out of his jeans.

I look up the time from the clock on the wall. Ten minutes past twelve. I rock Carl back and forth to wake him.

'Carl! Get up! It's ten past twelve!'

'Alright fuck's sake, give me a minute!' he shouts back in a daze.

I get my shoes from the hall and put them on. Then I realise the state of my clothes. Scuffs and stains are what cover my jeans, and my top has started to smell.

All my clothes are in my own house which is clearly a no-go zone. I need to buy some more today.

We get ready and leave the house for a quarter to one.

We drive to Boucher Road which is a large shopping exchange. It would put you to mind of an industrial estate that has been taken over by large retail stores.

We drive down a great length of the road and turn up into one of the back roads called Wildflower Way. This particular back road is thickly lined each side by trees which makes the road seem even narrower than it already is. The road is empty and drowned in shadow.

We park up on the curb and wait. We wait in silence, getting more anxious with each car passing the road behind us, thinking the next could be the one to turn into the road.

A black BMW surprises us from the other end of the road. It drifts slowly down the road and parks about fifty yards in front of our car. We get out and carefully make our way towards it.

As we get closer, two men get out and walk around to the front of the car to meet us.

'Hey, Carl, I'm Willy's guy.'

Carl greets him, extending his hand out to the tallest man.

The man then takes and twists Carl's arm, pushing his face down onto the car's bonnet. The other man grips me and pushes me up against the side of the car. They both begin to pat me and Carl down. A third man exits the car from the back seat. He is a small, skinny man wearing a purple shirt.

'Can never be too careful,' he says as he walks to the front of the car where his men finish patting us down and release us from their grips. He has a very strong Liverpool accent.

'No shit,' Carl says, straightening his jacket.

'So, Willy tells me you boys are interested in a large order, that right? Name's Chester by the way.'

'Yeah, that's right,' I cut in before Carl.

'You sure you can afford it?' Chester asks, looking sideways at us.

'We're middlemen. Our employer wants to remain anonymous, he can't be seen to be associated with such...trade. I'm sure as a businessman, you can understand,' I state, improvising. I hope Carl just follows my lead.

'Four keys of white, ring a bell? Tell your boss it will set him back a hundred and twenty thousand,' Chester says.

'That's what we're after,' Carl answers.
Chester's eyes bounce between me and Carl, his pause seemingly lingering.

'Tonight suit you both?' he asks.

'We'll have to make a few phone calls, but shouldn't be a problem,' Carl balances our story.

'Good. You'll have to make your way over to the Liverpool docks by four in the morning.'

'Alright, that's no problem,' Carl says.

'Give me your number, I'll text you the details later.'

I offer up my number and Chester notes it down on his phone.

We both wait for Chester to say more but he just turns and gets back into the car. His two henchmen then get back into the car and it slowly pulls away, leaving us standing on the footpath.

***

Shortly after the meet, we struggle to find a plane or ferry to Liverpool for tonight.

That's when I get an idea.

I call up Jim, the fairy.

That's the nickname everyone gave him as he is the captain of a ferry up in Larne. He does private trips for the right price and can bypass the authorities which is why he is, or at least was, used to smuggle stuff across the channel. I use the old pass-phrase from my Dublin days when I call him up. It still works. He agrees to a return journey for a thousand pounds.

We arrive in Larne around half-six in the evening. We enter the car park of the dock which is completely deserted.

We leave the car and walk up to the large white ferry. A man waits on the gangway for us with both arms rested on the support chains. It's Jim. He is an old, weathered man with white hair and dark dirty stubble. He has a slouched posture, covered in a stained fisherman's coat.

'Michael I take it?' he asks.

'Yeah, and this is my brother, Carl.'

'Alright, first thing's first. The money.'

I reach into my rucksack that I've brought along and grab a strapped bundle of cash and hand it over to him.

'It's all there,' I tell him.

Despite this, Jim undoes the strap and begins to count it in front of us. Once he has it all counted, he bundles it all back together and stuffs it messily into his coat pocket.

'Ya can never be too careful. You'd be surprised how many boys try to squeeze ya outta fifty or even a hundred quid. Anyway, c'mon, let's get going,' Jim says.

We board the ship and seat ourselves in the club lounge. Jim made it clear to us that we can help ourselves to drinks which Carl goes off in search for up by the bar area.

The lounge is very modern and tidy with white leather everywhere, combined with stainless steel trimmings.

The dark tide smoothly slides outside beyond the glass wall of the lounge, bouncing back our reflections from the bright lighting inside.

Carl comes back with two glasses and a premium bottle of whiskey. We sit down in one of the booths and I put the rucksack up on the table. I open the zip and pull the bag open.

'It look legit to you?' I ask Carl.

Carl leans forward to look down into the bag.

The bag is packed full of cash.

He puts his hand inside and moves the money around, revealing the fact that only the top row is the only row of real money.

The rest is newspaper trimmings, cut to precision and bound in the same way as the real money.

'They can't get a good look at the bag or they'll have it figured out right away,' he says.

'Right, so what do you think we should do?'

'What was your plan?' he asks.

'Misdirection,' I say, pouring myself a glass of whiskey. 'How?'

'One of us needs to distract them. They ask for the cash, we give them a glimpse but nothing else. After that, we ask to see the coke. When we know where it is, one of us draws the attention while the other sneaks closer to the coke to figure out a way of getting away with it.'

'And what if we can't?'

'We have to. The more time we need to figure that out, the more creative the distraction has to be,' I say after drinking half my glass of whiskey.

'Well, you were always the creative one,' Carl says, drinking straight from the whiskey bottle.

'I'll be the distraction if you can handle the rest,' I offer.

'I'll do it.'

***

The journey takes around eight hours.

We arrive in Liverpool shortly after three o'clock.

We pay Jim an extra three hundred to wait for us. The clock is ticking.

We are just about to leave the ferry when I outstretch the rucksack to Carl.

'Take this a second, I need to make a call.'

Carl takes the rucksack.

'What ya mean? Now?'

'Yes now. I'll be two seconds,' I return inside the ferry to get some privacy, despite Carl being visibly pissed off.

I come back after making my phone call and step out into the hazy rain of the Liverpool docks.

The rain hits my face like an ice-cold spray and it doesn't stop.

I take the lead in the long walk up the abandoned docks, fighting against the intense gales and rain with Carl following tight in behind me to use me as a wind blocker.

The haze of the rain is only visible under the amber lights that stretch along the docks. The smell of the sea does little to improve the situation but at least the place is empty.

Leaving the docks, we take position outside a couple of houses by the roadside, giving the impression we are from the houses when we get picked up by a taxi.

We take the journey to an industrial estate that Chester gave me the name of in his text message. When we are dropped off, the rain hasn't eased too much. We walk along a beaten-up road, debris and potholes stretch its entire length. I take my phone out of my pocket, unzip my coat and shield it inside to stop the screen from getting wet. It proves tricky trying to key in the address this way but there is no shelter around. The location marker shows up on the screen. We are very close. The warehouse is only five hundred yards ahead, up on our right.

We come upon an industrial stretch of the road, warehouses lining either side of the road behind metal fences, complete with barbed wire at the top. We hasten our walk to a light jog until we reach the steel shutters of the warehouse marked on my phone's map.

'Is this it?' Carl asks, shouting over the noise of the wind and rain.

'This is where my phone says it is!'

'You sure it's right?'

'Well, it's the address that guy Chester texted to me.'

A loud creaking sound interrupts our conversation. We look down to our left to see that the steel fire door has swung open, with a man leaning out of the building, looking directly at us.

'In here!' he shouts.

We rush inside to escape the elements, the steel door swings and thuds closed behind us.

'We're up ahead,' the man says, pointing to a door at the far end of the small corridor which we have ended up in.

The man stays where he is, watching us. I take the lead towards the door, opening it and stepping out into a large, baron warehouse drenched in darkness.

Without warning, all of the bright lights overhead blare bright, turning the warehouse into a burning white. When my eyes adjust, I see two SUVs parked over by the steel shutter me and Carl were on the other side of just moments ago.

'The O'Connell brothers,' a man's voice echoes.

My vision still hasn't fully returned to make an I.D on the man stepping forward from a small crowd by the SUVs.

'I like your style boys, go big or go home. None of this petty dealing shit. I'd like to meet your employer to discuss business maybe. If you could put me in touch?'

'Your name is?' Carl asks sceptically.

'Ridley, I run this operation,' he says confidently, his scouse accent even heavier than that of Chester.

'This is more of a side venture for our employer. He's more of a legit businessman these days,' Carl answers.

My vision finally adjusts and I can see Ridley stood in front of his henchmen.

He is in his forties, with broad shoulders and bleached, spiky hair along with a tan suit.

'Hmm, still. Business is all about networking. I'm very much looking to expand the business into new markets, such as your neck of the woods.'

58

'I'll speak to him personally when we get back. Can we see the product?' Carl asks.

'Can I see the money?' Ridley asks.

Carl unzips the rucksack and walks towards Ridley, Ridley's henchmen move around to get a better vantage point on Carl. Ridley reaches out for the rucksack as it comes within reach but Carl withdraws it, clutching the sides shut again.

'Can we see the product?' Carl asks again.

Ridley gives a look of disdain, scrunching his face up so much that he sniffs. He exhales in a sigh, relaxing, returning his disposition to calm once more before looking to one of his henchmen.

'Open it,' he commands.

The henchman goes to the boot of one of the SUVs and opens it. Inside is a stack of small white bags. The henchman takes one and brings it back to Ridley. Ridley makes a small tear in the bag with some of the powdery contents spilling onto the floor.

He offers it to Carl.

Carl takes it with his free hand, squeezing it. He then hands it to me. I scoop out a fingertip of powder and test it on my tongue, rubbing the remainder between my lips.

'You sure you've got the full amount there cowboy? Bag looks kinda light for a hundred gees,' Ridley says to Carl.

'Don't you worry, it's all here,' Carl fires back.

'Well then give it here and you can start packing your stuff into that bag. We've more in the Jeeps. I'd say two rucksacks each should be enough to take all the powder.'

My heart sinks during Ridley's last sentence. I keep staring at the bag of coke in my hand, looking for a way out.

'You know what..,' I say, enticing Ridley's attention. 'I think I'll stop wasting any time and give our employer a call right now. This stuff is unreal. Seriously, we never get anything this pure across the water.'

Ridley gestures with open hands. 'Why not, please feel free.'

'You mind if we pop back here for some privacy?' I ask, pointing with my thumb behind me towards the door of the corridor we came from.

'Go ahead,' Ridley says.

As I turn, I put my hand on Carl's shoulder, ushering him along with me. We go over beside the door we came in and I take out my phone.

'What are you doing?' Carl whispers.

I enter in random digits then pretend to call a number by putting the phone up to my ear.

'When you hear these doors go in, get that SUV. I'll get the shutters,' I whisper back, tilting my head towards the phone as I speak, to give the illusion of a phone call to Ridley and his preying eyes.

'There's about six guys around him, they're all bound to have guns,' Carl says.

'But they won't all be aiming at us, trust me.'

A loud bang echoes throughout the warehouse.

'What the fuck is that?' I hear one of the henchmen shout.

All of our attentions direct to the rear of the warehouse where the sound of even more bangs follow along with the pounding of boots.

'Police! Stay where you are!' A voice shouts as armed police storm the warehouse floor.

Ridley and his henchmen draw their weapons and start firing at the police.

In the ensuing chaos, me and Carl draw our own pistols from our belts and sprint for the SUVs. Ridley and his men start to move away from the SUVs which are taking much of the fire from the police, with the windows shattering from the bullets.

Carl rushes ahead of me, dropping the rucksack and shooting wildly at the henchmen.

I divert my path from Carl's and head towards the shutter controls. I hear the sound of bullets hitting and bouncing off the SUV next to me as I hit the button to raise the shutter.

I turn and I am blinded by the headlights that burst into life right in front of my eyes. Looking over the bonnet I see that Carl has already assumed control of the SUV.

I rush around to the passenger door and let the shutter raise automatically.

I put my hand on the door handle but feel a sharp pain in my side before the pain shifts to my other side as I'm forced into the door of the SUV.

I drop my gun from the collision.

I grab my attacker in a headlock and we wrestle to the ground. It's very frantic and primal, doing what we can to hurt each other, to find a way to win. We scratch, claw and bite to get to a dominant position. I get a grip of his neck, choking him, his grip loosens on me and I get to my knees over him, pressing down harder on his neck.

'Michael, let's go!' I hear Carl shout from the driver's seat.

I bash my fists off the henchman's face as hard and as fast as I can, so much that I know he won't stop me from getting away.

I get up and get into the SUV just as the police close in. Carl puts his foot down and we race out of the warehouse and onto the small roads of the industrial estate.

We ram the tail end of a police car blocking our way, sending it spinning into the footpath. Picking up speed again, I check behind us, we aren't being followed.

Carl takes us out of the industrial estate and onto the motorway.

I've never heard an engine roar so violently, with Carl pushing the vehicle to its limits, keeping it constantly over a hundred miles per hour on these roads which are mostly straight runs.

It takes us half the time to arrive back at the docks where, to our relief, the ferry is still waiting. Carl parks as close to the ferry as possible without driving into the sea.

We unload the boot in a blind panic. Jim meets us on the gangway as we rush back and forth from the ferry to the SUV.

'What the fuck is going on?' Jim shouts.

'Just help us!' Carl shouts at him whilst rushing past with the small bags of cocaine.

'Hang on! Wait a fucking minute!' Jim shouts back, pointing with his finger.

I have no time for this. On my return journey from the SUV, I make the point to Jim.

'Listen, you can either help us or not. Either way, in the next few minutes the cops or a gang with guns will be coming through those gates. So help us load or get this boat moving!'

'You wee fucking bastards! I want extra for this!' he scolds as he disappears back into the ferry.

Carl and I give the SUV one final sweep before leaving it.

We get back on board the ferry just as it starts to move away from the dock.

We find an old metal locker on board and steal it to use as a storage container for the coke.

Carl disappears after we fill the locker full. I was expecting him to help move it but I guess I have to struggle on my own with it. It was quite light when we took it out of the small cloakroom but now it weighs a ton as if it were filled with bricks.

Well, in a way it kind of is. It takes all my strength to drag it back to the club lounge where we can keep a safe eye on it. I regularly have to stop to catch a break and give my burning muscles time to cool down, then I'm straight back to trailing it. The corners of the locker scratch into the wooden floor, leaving large gorges and marks. Hopefully, Jim won't notice them before we leave or he'll want extra to pay for the damage and we need every penny.

I trip into the club lounge, narrowly avoiding the falling locker as it crashes down beside me, inches from my right leg. It makes such a loud smash, like a collapsing wall.

I hear Carl's faint mumble, I must've disturbed him.

When I get to my feet, I see that he is asleep in one of the cubicles, laid across the length of the white leather seat.

'Lazy fuck,' I mutter to myself.

I take a look at the locker, with half of it in the lounge and the other still in the hallway. Ah, fuck it. It'll do. I'm too tired to do any more. I walk down the lounge, past Carl, and take the last cubicle.

I take off my coat and roll it up in a bundle. Falling onto the seating, my coat acts as my pillow. It takes a while to drift off, I lay there, staring at the imperfections in the ceiling. I trace every crack and every blemish in the paint.

I wonder where Layla makes her bed tonight.
Does she have the luxury of a pillow?
Has she eaten?
I'm coming, honey. Daddy's coming to get you from the bad men.
That's what I keep telling myself. This boat can't move fast enough.

DAY FOUR

Carl's voice calls out and I fight to open my unwilling eyes. 'Michael, Michael get up. We're home.'

I sit up in my seat, rubbing my stinging eyes as I battle to open them.

Everything slowly comes into focus. The lights are still on in the lounge but appear dim against the growing daylight coming in through the glass wall. Carl takes a seat and puts his boots on, I see Jim beyond him by the door as he kicks the locker that still lays half in, half out.

'Ya stealing one of my fucking lockers too ya bastards?' he scorns.

'I'll pay you for it,' I tell him in an exhausted breath, the words coming out more like muttered syllables.

I grab my coat off my seat, struggling to get my arm into a twisted sleeve. I give up and tie it around my waist instead when I get to my feet.

Jim disappears from the doorway and I meet Carl beside the locker.

'Couldn't ya have picked something with wheels?' Carl jokes.

'Just lift it, I'm way too tired for this,' I insist.

We carry the locker off the ferry and over beside the car. It's the small hours of the morning, I remember glancing at my phone on the way out and seeing what I think was almost noon.

The cold, blustery winds cut through my clothes and pierce an invisible dagger of ice into my chest.

'Well it's not fitting in there,' Carl says, comparing the measurement by eye.

It was obviously too big to put in the boot and too wide to feed through the car.

I open the boot up in a rage, push the locker over till it crashes flat on the ground and begin to load the small bags into the boot.

I notice Jim approaching out of the corner of my eye but I don't give him my attention and continue to load the car angrily. The sound of Jim's boots pounding on the gravel gets right up next to us.

'Hey! I'm wanting extra for this, I nearly broke the anchor when we had to pull away in a panic. Then my locker. That's my boy's locker, he uses it when we go on trips.'

I ignore him.

Noticing this, Carl caters to Jim.

'Much you looking?' Carl asks.

'Pfft, at least three hundred.'

During my movements between the locker and the boot, I see Carl pulling out his wallet and handing money over to Jim. Jim counts it then starts to walk off just as I load the last bag and close the boot.

I see Carl tilting his head and looking inside the now, empty locker.

'Hey!' he calls out to Jim. Jim turns around. 'You can have your locker back!'

'Shove it up your hole!' Jim shouts back, giving Carl the middle finger.

We both get into the car and I start up the engine. The car kicks into life.

***

The moment we enter the front door of the house, I'm quick to offer some personal wisdom to Carl.

'Right, we need to hide the coke in the house. We can't leave it out there in the car. It's an easy target.'

'Well, I don't wanna keep it here for long. I'll start calling my guys soon to start shifting it. Maybe a couple of days will get it gone. They're all linked to big-time dealers.'

'OK.'

'OK, we put it all in the kitchen cupboards? Should hold it.'

'No, no. Never put it all in the same spot. If the place gets raided or someone busts in, you can lose it all at once. We'll spread it out. Maybe fill the cupboards in the kitchen and hide the rest in the shed outside,' I say.

'Right, well let's start getting it in,' Carl demands.

We bring the bags in from the car, all the while we watch the windows of the neighbours' houses for any movement of the blinds or curtains. We smuggle it all in like when we used to sneak beer crates into the house when mum and dad left over the summer holidays almost every year.

67

The neighbours are notorious touts so it was always treated like a covert operation, sneaking drink into the house whilst avoiding their watchful eyes.

It's finally all tucked away, just like we planned. Some in the kitchen and the rest in the shed outside.

I think we come to an unspoken agreement when we return to the living room and collapse on a sofa each. We only must have got a few hours sleep on the ferry home and now was as good a time as any to relax. A kind of reward for getting this far, the rest should be plain sailing.

I sink into the smaller sofa, having never found comfort like this before in my life. The transition to sleep feels almost instant until the bashing starts on the front door.

***

I spring off the sofa and stop dead when the bashing stops. It starts again, more violently than before, I can hear the door struggling to withstand the assault. Carl falls off his sofa from waking in a panic. We both stay low on the floor as the front blinds are open.

We edge towards the open living room door. The bashing continues and the clanking of metal indicates the weakening of the locks. This is it, they've found us. Do we break for it and try and get out the back? It means going out into the hall and then down through the kitchen. They'd spot us for sure. If we are lucky, they might bypass the living room and go for either the kitchen or upstairs. I still have the car keys in my pocket so we'd stand a chance of escape.

Before I could give it another moments thought, we hear the front door swinging in and hitting the small hall table beside it. My pulse races even faster and my fists clench. I see the worried look on my brother's face and I have never felt so responsible for his well-being.

I take charge by taking a stand and launching towards the hallway before Carl has time to act.

I crash into a man and start trying to wrestle him to the ground. It happens so quick I don't get a look at his face. He quickly grabs me in a headlock against his tan coloured jacket while I drive my shoulder into him, backing him up into a wall.

'Harry! Harry! It's us!' I hear Carl shout.

Uncle Harry? I think. The grip on my head loosens and I let go, looking up to see an old, greying man. My uncle who I hadn't seen in years. He hasn't aged well.

'What are you doing here?' he asks angrily.

'We had nowhere else to go,' Carl explains.

Harry's gaze turns on me.

'I heard about you and our little Layla. What's going on?'

'I'm trying to get her back.'

'That's a job for the police, not you.'

'And look how far they've got,' I say.

Harry fixes his scruffy hair and then goes to the broken door.

'You two change the locks? I was scared someone might be squatting here,' Harry asks.

'I left my key in the door,' Carl explains. 'Listen, you can't be here. It's a lot to explain but it's too dangerous.'

Harry fires Carl a haunting scorn.

'What are you on about? What could you possibly do to make matters any worse?' he asks, studying Carl, then looking to me. 'Awk, fuck. What is it?'

Carl sits him down in the living room and explains everything. Harry used to be a cop which is where he derives the authoritative nature from. He was always the solid, stable rock of the family who everyone would count on in a complicated or stressful situation.

He takes it quite well, better than I expected. He knows my past just as well as Carl but he never knew of my return to the country. I strayed away from contact with family and old friends in case word got around that I was back. I needed to stay in the shadows no matter what.

Carl goes off to get his key from the door and then to the toilet, giving me and Harry some privacy.

Harry leans in closer to me as we sit side by side on the sofa. 'Do you really think this plan is going to work?'

'It's gonna work,' I tell him.

'Well let's say you get the money. You go to the drop and meet your old boss. You really think it'll be a matter of forgive and forget? You swap the money over for Layla and you turn and walk happily away. You know this world better than me or Carl. How do you think this is really going to end?'

For the first time since the night of Layla's kidnap, I ponder on the unthinkable yet realistic take on my situation. What if he's right? What if my initial gut feelings were right? That this is the way it probably will end?

Carl comes back into the room and we fall silent again. Carl's gaze bounces between me and Harry.

'What is it? What's up?'

'Nothing,' I mutter, disheartened.

'I'm gonna start calling my guys and get this shit shifted quick.'

'Give me a ring when you're ready to start making drops. I'm going down to the shop,' I tell Carl.

'You taking the car?' Carl asks.

'Nah, I'm gonna walk. Could do with the air.'

'Watch no one spots you out walking around and calls the cops,' Carl says worriedly as I make my way out of the house.

I walk along the rain-drenched footpaths of the estate, running back over what Harry had said. What he had said about my plan. Are Carl and I deluding ourselves into thinking this story has a happy ending? I'm really starting to second guess everything we've done up to this point. Maybe Harry is right, maybe I should have got the cops involved. But would that have made my position any better as I stand right now?

I start to reason with myself, bringing myself back from the edge of insanity. The fact is we do have a plan. We have a way to get all of the money. Something I thought on that first night was impossible to do. But here we are, about to sell a mountain of stolen cocaine and take our earnings straight to Tommy. I don't know how else to play this out, and if there was another way I don't know if I would take it. I'm in control of this, I'm doing this on my terms and if it fails, the weight of blame will fall on my shoulders.

When I get outside the shop, I forgot what initial impulse there was to come here. I know there was something I wanted to buy, maybe a drink of sort, but my mind goes blank.

71

I look around the entrance of the shop. It seems quite busy with all of the people coming and going. Fear gets the best of me, the fear of being spotted or recognised. It would put everything we've achieved so far in jeopardy.

I turn my back on the shop, my freedom to roam, and head back to the house.

I turn into our street when my phone starts vibrating.

It's Carl calling.

'Hello.'

'Hey, where are you?'

'Top of the street, I'll be there in a minute.'

'Right, meet me at the car. We're dropping two bags over to this guy, Connal.'

'Right OK, bye.'

I walk up to and stand beside the car. I only have to wait a few seconds before Carl appears from the house, carrying a plastic supermarket bag with something heavy weighing it down.

'OK, get in,' Carl says, opening the electronic locks and walking around to the driver's door. We get into the car and he throws the bag behind us, into the back seat.

We start driving and I notice Carl has a very serious look on his face.

'When we get to this place, just follow my lead. You need to watch yourself,' he says.

'Where are we going?'

'It's a rough ass bar over in the west. These guys don't fuck about, they're savages. If they don't even like the look of you, they'll let you know.'

'Fuck 'em, I don't throw my eyes to the floor for anyone,' I tell Carl defiantly.

'See! That's what I'm talking about,' Carl shouts, gesturing with his hands. 'Keep it calm, we're here to do business. We're going here for Layla, OK?' he continues shouting until the mention of Layla's name and then quietens down.

We park in a street a few doors up from the pub.

As we walk up to it I see it's a very old, weathered pub. The wooden exterior is rotten and splintering, the paintwork is so faded I can only make out every other letter of the pub's name.

There are men outside smoking, which goes to show the kind of crowd it attracts. They are in their forties, in football jerseys and plastered in intimidating tattoo designs - one even has his bald head tattooed. They stop and glare at us as we enter the bar, brushing past them as they refuse to make way for me and Carl.

Once inside, it's clear this place is run under its own rules.

The air is thick with cigarette smoke, a far away jukebox box plays pop music from the eighties and the floor is sticky in every spot from spilt drinks. It's like a health and safety officer died and went to hell.

Carl leads the way, deeper into the bar. All of the patrons cast a suspicious eye on us, outsiders staining their patch. I try my best not to make any eye contact and keep close behind Carl. He walks up to the bartender. The bartender is a small, snake-like man with sunken cheekbones and a frail structure.

'You can tell Connal that Carl is here,' Carl says confidently to him as if he were someone of notability.

The bartender looks up from shining a large pint glass with a dirty white rag of cloth.

'You can tell him yourself, he's right over there,' the bartender says, directing his eyes and nodding towards the back of the bar.

We both look to see a young man in a tracksuit, with a shaved head and a half-grown goatee, surrounded by three of his friends, similar in description.
Carl and I make our way over. Connal and his friends turn in their seats to face us.

The screech of their wooden chairs scraping on the floor is an uncomfortable disturbance in the already tense atmosphere.

'Connal, you still interested in our deal?' Carl asks as we come to stop in front of his table of friends.

'Carl, nice to see ya mate. Ya haven't been in here in a long time have ya? Aye, what's the split again?'

'Seventy-thirty.'

'Mmm, it rings a bell but now that I hear it out loud. It doesn't seem quite right. So,' he says, cockily as he takes a drink of his beer, setting it gently back on the table. 'How about we make it sixty-forty. To me, of course.'

'Well that wasn't the deal,' Carl says, eyeing up his friends who look ready to pounce.

'This is the new deal,' Connal says with a smile.

Carl takes two steps forward, walking right in front of Connal's table and leaning down on it with both hands, staring at Connal. He then reaches out and calmly lifts up Connal's beer.

His friends immediately spring to their feet, pushing their chairs out from underneath them, again with that

74

screeching sound of wood scraping across the concrete floor.

I stay standing where I am, anticipating everyone's next move. Carl slowly starts drinking the beer right in front of him to Connal's disgust.

'Just because you're still Davey's favourite bitch, doesn't make you the big dick, Connal.'

Carl mockingly wipes the beer residue from his lips.

'Well how about I just take your fucking gear and your brother?' Connal shouts, getting to his feet as one of his friends closest to me, grabs me and puts a gun to my head.

Carl half turns to see what's going on and turns his attention back to Connal.

Carl takes his hands off the table and stands up straight, adjusting the collar on his jacket.

'Your other friend packing or is he the heavy muscle?' Carl asks, gesturing his head towards Connal's other friend to his left, who remains standing with his hands by his side.

Connal just smiles at Carl. I can make out Carl smiling back, from adjusting his collar, he swiftly slides his hand down inside his jacket and a loud bang rattles my eardrums.

A puff of smoke comes from Carl's jacket where something seems to protrude. Connal's idle friend falls backwards into a table. I struggle against his other friend's grip who holds on and keeps the gun tight to my skull.

Carl pulls a pistol from his jacket and aims it at Connal who raises his hands and cowers his head down.

'Tell your mate to let my brother go, right fucking now!' Carl shouts.

'Let him go! Let him go!' Connal commands his friend.

I feel his friend's grip loosen and I take the gun off him and aim it around the bar for any ambushes. Everyone stays stone still with the mood shifting, the pop music from the jukebox remains upbeat.

'Michael, get the door,' Carl instructs.

Connal's injured friend lays on the floor groaning, holding his stomach where he has been shot.

'He'll live,' Carl tells Connal over the groans.

We both move slowly towards the front door, keeping our guns aimed high and ready. No one in the bar even looks shaken up from the events unfolding, kind of like it was commonplace.

We don't rush, we walk slowly until my back hits the wooden double doors and we ram them open and sprint out into the street.

'Go go go!' I hear Carl shout behind me, running down to the car.

We get in and I spot the patrons come flooding out of the bar as Carl tries to start the car, but it won't start.

'C'mon! c'mon!' Carl shouts in frustration, turning the key over and over again but the engine won't start.

The patrons spot us trying to get away and start running down towards the car.

'They're coming,' I tell Carl, locking my door and cocking my gun in my lap.

They bash into the car, trying to get inside by pulling violently on the handles whilst shouting at us at the top of their voices. They try every door of the car and even start to climb onto the bonnet.

The man on the bonnet sits on his rear and starts kicking the windscreen with his boots. The engine roars into life after countless attempts to start it. Carl throws the car into reverse and we race backwards, scaring away those at the back of the car. We slam into a stationary mini cooper which then sends its alarm ringing. The man on the bonnet holds on to the windscreen wipers, still trying to kick the windscreen in, a crack appears with his last boot. Carl shifts into first gear and floors it, turning onto the main road. We lose the crowd from the bar but the man in front still holds on to the wipers.

Carl slams on the breaks about fifty yards up the road from the bar and the man falls off, taking one of the wipers with him.

We take a sharp left and disappear through a series of side streets.

'If these are the kind of friends you've got, we're fucked!' I tell Carl.

'Fuck it, we'll go see Dave,' Carl says.

'Who is that?' I ask.

'The top guy. The guy above Connal.'

We make another stop on the way home. Carl goes into the house alone and comes back out within fifteen-minutes.

He tells me that everything has been straightened out and that Connal will be put in his place, we have a deal.

***

When we get into the house, I go to the kitchen and open the fridge for a drink. It's almost empty already. We haven't got any groceries since our last shopping trip, which involved me being hunted around the store by the cops. Nothing in the fridge apart from a few half-drunken beers and a carton of milk. I take the milk out and go to the cupboard to get a glass. On second thoughts, I only want a sip, so I take off the lid and drink from the bottle and lean against the worktop. I hear a knock at the door but I ignore it, leaving it to either Harry or Carl to get it. I take another drink from the milk bottle as the door knocks again, heavier and more aggressive than the first time.

'For fuck's sake, what's your problem!' I say out loud as I straighten up and walk into the hall, towards the front door.

The first bullets hit the wall beside me before I react and sprawl down onto the floor. It's then that I see the barrel of the rifle being poked through the shattered glass of the door, knocking away the rest of the glass still obstructing their view.

I scramble like a dog on my hands and knees, right up to the door, right underneath the barrel of the gun. I look up at it as the last of the glass is bashed away and it falls on top of me.

He tries to open the door but I brace my weight against the door, stopping it from opening more than a couple of inches.

I hear Carl returning shots from the living room.

The barrel hanging over me points down and fires a burst of shots - all of them miss to my joy. A couple narrowly avoided hitting my feet. I reach up out of desperation and grab the barrel with both hands, pushing it up towards the ceiling. I stretch up onto my feet to meet my attacker face to face. He's wearing a balaclava but I can see his gritted teeth exposed from the mask, struggling to out-wrestle me for the gun. He pulls the trigger and the gun jumps in our hands, with neither of us letting go. The barrel becomes burning hot but I dare not let go. I spot

78

some sharp shards of glass that still stand in the broken door window.

I sharply pull the gun inside, along with the guy's arms. I snap them down on top of the sharp glass, impaling his left arm on one of the larger shards. He screams in agony and his grip loosens on the gun. I spin the gun around, point it to his head and pull the trigger. I hear a loud bang come from behind me.

I turn to see the back door in the kitchen open from the garden. Another masked man steps inside with a pistol. I charge towards him, I see him panic.

He rushes to the hallway door and closes it in front of me, seconds before I reach it. I don't hesitate, I boot the door open again, I even feel the door hit the masked man as I follow through with my kick.

The door swings open to reveal the man landing on his back. I'm quicker to draw, spilling his blood on the kitchen floor. Glass and the wooden fittings of the kitchen start to break apart and skip into the air, the sound is deafening with the windows also shattering amidst an onslaught of gunfire coming from the garden. I back up and shut the kitchen door.

'Michael!' I hear my brother's voice shout.

I turn around to see Carl carrying a drowsy Harry out of the living room and into the hall over one of his shoulders.

'He got hit, he's in shock,' Carl explains under a heavy breath.

'Get him up the stairs!' I shout.

Bullets start to flood in through the front door, ripping into the walls of the hall. I run and slide on my knees into the front door, hitting it with a thud. Carl drags Harry up the stairs while the bullets continue to pour in.

I put my gun up and point it out of the broken window of the door, shooting blindly to cover their retreat. I shoot until the clip empties. Ahead of me, the door to the kitchen swings open again and two masked men come to a stop in the doorway, raising their rifles. I jump forward to the cover of the stairs when their bullets come for me. I scramble up the stairs, losing my footing in the panic. I hear the front door being kicked in. As I get halfway up, the pictures on the wall beside me come crashing onto the stairs at my feet, with holes being torn into every surface on the trail for me.

I get to the top of the stairs and start to look for Carl and Harry.

'Carl! Carl! Where are you?'

I run to the main bedroom and look inside, it's empty, or are they hiding in here? I don't have time to look, every second counts. Footsteps start to creep up the stairs, I freeze on the spot in a blind spot of the stairs, thinking. How am I going to take them out? How many of these guys are there? I'm still trying to figure out in my head who they are. Are they Tommy's guys, has Tommy decided on just wiping me out? It could be Chester too, has he come here for what we stole from him? Shit, the stash is all downstairs. We can't hide up here and let them take run of the house. We can't afford to let them get away with it, Layla can't afford it.

The footsteps slowly get closer to the top of the stairs.

The bathroom door facing the stairs swings open and a blast of gunfire erupts from it towards the stairs. The door then swings closed again after the flurry and a barrage of bullets riddle the door.

I move up towards the top of stairs as the bathroom door edges open again to return fire. I turn the corner and punch one of the two masked men standing there, he starts to fall backwards down the stairs as his friend turns his attention on me. He shakes violently as he is hit by several bullets and he too, falls backwards, rolling down the stairs.

I pick up a rifle that one of the men have dropped, pointing it down the stairs, waiting for someone to appear over the two bodies that lay at the foot of them. No one shows, but I can hear them down there.

I hear the bathroom door swinging open.

Carl emerges from the bathroom, checking each way with his rifle.

'Where's Harry?' I ask.

'He's in there,' he says as I go past him, into the bathroom.

I find my uncle Harry unconscious in the bathtub, his t-shirt soaked in blood at the stomach.

'Shit! Is he still breathing?' I ask Carl as I check Harry's pulse.

'He's still alive but we need to get him to the hospital.'

Just as Carl says that, bullets hit the roof in front of him. I duck down beside the bath and I see him take shelter against the wall beside the stairs. I check my bullet count then slide the magazine back in.

'We've gotta get downstairs,' I tell Carl.

Carl nods at me with gritted teeth and an intense look on his face.

'Then let's fucking go!' he shouts, spinning around the wall and storming down the stairs, I rush to get his back.

We move swiftly down the stairs, vulnerable, in the open.

We get down to the hall with no trouble, no ambush. Carl splinters off into the living room, I set my sights on the kitchen, moving towards the door which is slightly ajar, covered in bullet holes.

As I take each step, I walk on broken glass, splinters of wood and wood dust, I try my best to not make any sound. I put my hand against the door, thinking about slowly pushing it open to ease my nerves. I take a deep breath and grip the rifle tighter.

I smash the door open using my shoulder and take aim. I'm greeted by thick grey smoke that chokes me. Forcing to keep my eyes open, I see the kitchen is on fire., no one is here and the back door has been left open.

I go straight to the cupboards where we stashed some of the coke. I open the cupboard doors and my heart sinks at the sight I'm greeted with. They've taken it all, not even a trace remains. I slam the doors shut in a rage, breaking the hinges off one of the doors.

The shed, it's the biggest stash. I hope they haven't thought to check there. If they have, it's all over.

I go straight outside and across the grass to the shed. I go inside, throwing my rifle down in my rage as I tear junk out of the way, throwing it recklessly behind me in search for any white bags. I put them here myself, where the fuck are they?

I dig the whole way to the back of the shed, there they are. Finally, we have some luck. I go back to the house, the fire in the kitchen has grown larger, taking up half the kitchen now.

'Carl!' I shout, going towards the living room.
I open the door and go into the living room.

An intense heat makes me squint my face and turn away. I take a step out into the hall again to look in. The entire room is engulfed in bright red flames as most of the smoke billows out of the broken windows.

I close the door again, where is Carl?

'Carl!' I shout again.

'Up here! C'mon, give me a hand!' I hear him call from upstairs.

I go up and meet him in the bathroom, trying to drag Harry out of the bathtub.

'Give me a hand,' he asks.

I grab a hold of Harry and help Carl drag him out of the bathtub and onto his feet. He's still unconscious so we take an arm each over our shoulders.

'We've gotta get out of here and get him to the hospital,' Carl says.

'They found the coke in the kitchen but we still have a stash in the shed,' I tell Carl.

'Fuck! Right, we'll figure it out later. Right now we need to deal with Harry.'

We get down the stairs to the front door but I stop.

'What are you doing?' Carl asks, annoyed that I've stopped.

'I'll meet you in the car, I need to put the fire out.'

'Michael, you can't. It's too far gone.'

'No, I won't let mum and dad's house burn to the ground,' I go to leave Harry's side but I feel Carl's hand stretch across and grip my shoulder tightly.

'Let it go,' Carl tells me.

I pull against his grip but he holds on.

'Let it go! Let it go,' Carl says with his tone turning softer.

I take my eyes off the walls of the house and focus them on the path ahead of the front garden. I help Carl take Harry out to the car which has remained untouched.

We throw Harry into the back seat. Carl gets in the back seat beside him and I go around the car to the driver's door. I take one last look at our parents' house, smoking pouring out from it and the flames now visible in the hall. Concerned neighbours have started edging down the street towards us.

All of the gunfire must have scared them all off to the top of the street.

Distant sirens start to ring out.

It is only a fifteen-minute drive to the hospital but I reckon I can do it in eight. The coke, I need to get it now, we can never come back here. I open the boot to the protests of Carl.

'What are you doing?' he shouts after me.

We need to pack up the coke now.

I leave the boot open and run back through the house to the back garden.

I hear a car door slamming behind me and once I get to the shed, Carl is right behind me. We both carry all the bags in one go using a wheelbarrow that has been hidden in the shed. We frantically throw the bags into the boot whilst neighbours and passers-by watch with interest and horror at the situation. We slam the boot closed and get into the car.

From memory, we only stashed a quarter in the kitchen so that's all we are missing, but we will have to make it up somehow. I take off down the street and floor it as we reach the large roundabout, narrowly missing oncoming cars.

'He's going cold and white!' Carl shouts from the back seat.

'Keep pressure on his stomach!' I shout back.

I race to catch the green light at the junction to the carriageway. The tail of the car swings out as I slide it around the bend, but I bring it back under control. I weave in and out of cars, hitting eighty on this stretch which is limited to fifty.

We reach the hospital in around nine minutes, I turn up into the hospital grounds when Carl's phone starts to ring.

'It's Willy,' Carl tells me.

'Put it on speaker,' I tell him before he answers.

I hear his phone beep and then Willy's paranoid voice comes through. 'Carl! What the fuck did you do man?'

'What are you talking about?' Carl plays dumb.

'Chester and his guys are looking for you. I had to tell them where you lived, I had to.'

'Really? I've been out all day. What do they want?'

'You better get down to here now. He's coming back here with his guys. I don't know what the fuck you did but you better come down and straighten this out or it's going to be my fucking head on a pike!'

Willy hangs up and the call ends.

I pull up outside the doors of A&E.

'Get him in there,' I say to Carl.

'Where are you going?' Carl asks, pulling Harry out of the car and coming to the window.

'C'mon, park it up and let's go,' Carl says.

'I'll be back in a minute, need to find a space, I can't park here,' I tell him.

Carl takes Harry inside. I spin the car around and speed out of the hospital grounds.

***

I drive to Carl's apartment block and hide the bags of coke inside a bin, right outside the doors of the block.

Sort of an insurance thing in case anything goes wrong.

I throw in one of the pistols on top, the Glock. I also manage to squeeze one of the rifles in too, it's a tight fit but that will have to do. The rest will have to stay in the boot of the car. I take the other pistol from the bag of guns and stuff it into the glove box of the car before putting the bag in the boot again. I take a look around for a final check in case anyone is watching but it looks clear.

I get back on the main roads and try to retrace the route I went on with Carl to find Willy's place. I get on to what I think is the right road. It's only when I see the sign of a Chinese takeaway, that I realise I'm on the right road.

'Wan Wee Cok'; either it's owned by a local guy with a dirty sense of humour or it's a very unfortunate Chinese name.

I drive up to Willy's but as I do, I see two black cars park right outside. I swing across and park on the other side of the road.

I stop, turn off the engine and watch.

A gang of men exit the cars, amongst them, I spot Chester. I take the pistol out of the glove box and check the magazine. It's full.

There's at least eight of them that I saw go inside. There's too many of them to get too up close. The maths doesn't add up in my favour. Still, I can't let them just walk away, I won't.

My mind races looking for an answer. They won't spend too long inside, not if they're smart. They just shot up and torched a house, anyone could've got their plates. I know I'll need to give them an answer as soon as they come back out those doors, then it hits me.

I tug at the bottom of my t-shirt, pulling it apart, stretching it until it finally rips.

I pull a strip around the bottom and rip it off, leaving me with a make-shift belly top. I roll up the torn off rag and get out of the car.

I run across the busy road and move along the line of parked cars, keeping low. I get behind one of the black cars, looking up through the windows at the doors, no one there.

I open the petrol cap of the car and stuff my rag inside it. I lean against the car, waiting for the door of Willy's to open.

Every time a line of cars pass, I pretend I am checking the rear tire before popping back up again. I hear the heavy wooden doors creak open. I peak up through the windows of the car to see Chester's men coming out. I don't wait for the sight of Chester, I take my lighter out and set light to the rag and then hurry my way back down the road, keeping low and keeping tight to the row of cars.

I cut in and hide at the rear of a Mercedes.

I peak out again to watch them get into the cars. They all get in the cars and they start to pull away from the curb. I can see the fire of the rag hanging from the rear car as it moves.

A loud pop rings out before the car explodes into flames.

The force of the explosion blows out the windows of nearby parked cars.

The first car stops and they all get out, going to the burning car.

I take my chance.

I take the pistol out of my trousers and edge closer from behind the cover of the parked cars with people running scared, away from the scene. I get close, real close. I stand up and start shooting. I drop the closest man with the first two shots. The rest go astray before I take cover again.

Bullets ricochet off the car I hide behind. I crawl on my hands and knees to the front of the car before emerging again. I gun down Chester's biggest man, then I catch Chester in the leg before he drops and disappears from view behind the burning car. I start walking with purpose towards where he dropped.

Checking my bullets, I slide the clip back in and cock the gun. I come around the burning car in the middle of the road to see Chester desperately trying to crawl away. Suddenly, a loud gunshot makes me take cover as it hits the burning car next to me.

'You shouldn't have fucked with the wrong guys!' I hear a voice shout.

I watch Chester crawl further away, then a man appears beside him, facing me. It's Willy.

'You little bastard!' he shouts, taking aim at me with his large shotgun.

I scramble to my feet and run. I hear the shot go off but it must've missed because I didn't feel anything, I'm still on my feet running. I hear another three shots go off behind me, each one getting more distant. I get to my car, get in and put it into reverse.

I reverse half the length of the road before stopping to turn. I get as far away as I can in any direction that is open.

My blood races through my veins and my mind is working overtime with all the adrenaline coursing through my system. I lower my window to get the cold breeze at my face to cool down. The humid air makes it hard to catch a breath. With no cars on my tail, I start to ease off the accelerator, driving at the road's limit.

Just as I start to settle down, my stomach sinks and my heart jumps at the sound of a police siren behind me. There in my rearview mirror, I spot the flashing lights of a police car closing in from behind. My foot slams back down on the accelerator before jumping to the brake pedal, the car shunts when I take a sharp turn.

Building up speed again, the engine getting louder and louder, I check every mirror. My eyes bounce from the wing mirrors to the rearview mirror and then back again, only getting brief glimpses of the clear, straight road ahead. My eyes stop and focus on the rearview mirror with interest and horror at the sight of a second police car joining the chase.

A glimpse of blue catches the corner of my sight, but it's already too late. I crash right into the side of a blue car emerging from a side street. Obviously, he wasn't looking at the road either.

The crash rocks me around in the car but luckily I had my seat belt on. I can see the front of my car is badly damaged, with the bonnet visibly bent up towards the middle. I'd imagine that both of the headlights as well as the grill are smashed to bits too.

The other driver throws his hands around and I can faintly hear him ranting inside his car when I go to reverse. The police cars stop right behind me as I'm reversing, but I don't stop. In fact, I speed up, ramming one of them to create space behind me.

The police in the second car get out and draw their guns on me. I duck down in my seat and change gear, throwing it into first and taking off. I hear the popping sounds in the body of the car as bullets hit it. I slowly rise in my seat to better see the road now that I'm far enough away but right ahead, a police land rover turns down into the road.

I stop the car in the middle of the road. I turn in my seat to look at the road behind me. There are no side streets to aid my escape, it's a straight stretch of road. One way in, one way out. The two police cars move off again, coming for me. The land rover ahead keeps coming too.

That's when I spot it, on the side of the road.

A small alleyway up the side of two houses.

I get out, not looking either left or right, my tunnel vision for the alleyway, I sprint as hard and as fast as my tired body will do it.

I've never moved so fast, my arms and shoulders thrusting and swinging with the run, my feet hitting the ground for mere split seconds, it almost feels like they barely touch the ground at all. I'm there, I've got it, I'm about to put my first foot onto the pavement when I feel myself behind hit from behind, slamming my back backwards, the next thing I see is the grey sky above before my shoulders and the back of my head make contact with the bonnet of one of the police cars.

When the car comes to a stop seconds after hitting me, I slide off the bonnet, slumping onto the road. By some miracle, there is no pain, I hit the car in just the right way, which is a strange thing to say but for the drama of the event, I escaped unscathed. I stay still on the ground though. I know I'm not going anywhere so I put on the act of being badly hurt, hoping they will take me to get checked out in the hospital before locking me up. That way I would still have a small chance of escape.

'Stay still, the paramedics are on their way,' a young policewoman instructs as she keeps watch over me.

The rest of the cops move to seal off the road.

The rough gravel of the road starts to become comforting, all I can do right now is wait. All of the guns are in the boot of the car, it's only going to get worse when they eventually get around to searching it.

It's another fifteen-minutes until the paramedics arrive. They put me onto a stretcher after a quick check of my condition. They tell the police that I will have to be examined at the hospital before I am admitted into custody.

The young policewoman joins me in the back of the ambulance alongside one of the paramedics. It's a very bumpy ride, the ringing of the sirens contribute to an oncoming of what must be travel sickness.

For the entire duration of the ride, both the paramedic and policewoman stay silent, stone-faced, focused on a certain spot on the floor that I'm unable to see to deduce its appeal. When the doors of the ambulance open again, it takes a few seconds for my eyes to adjust to the bright light.

I'm taken out of the ambulance and that's when I see that the other cops have also made it to the hospital to be my personal escort. They wheel me inside, the pain of the headache starts to affect the back of my neck making it stiff and sore, so I just lay down flat, watching the long, stretched lights of the hospital ceiling pass overhead as we travel deeper into the hospital.

We stop at the A&E department, they leave me pushed up against one of the walls with two of the policemen standing guard of me. I tilt my head and see the other two cops, along with the paramedics, at the reception desk explaining my case.

I wonder if this is the same hospital I took Harry and Carl to, are they still here?

I don't even know if Harry is OK.

My shortest ever wait in A&E is over in what seemed like less than ten minutes. I'm wheeled into a private room and kept on the stretcher. A nurse comes into the room, a small, soft-faced lady in her fifties.

'Can you please wait outside? The doctor is on his way over from the main building,' she asks the police and paramedics in a very friendly and kind voice.

They all leave as the nurse closes a window in the room and adjusts the angle of a seat by the bed.

Our eyes meet briefly and she gives me a gentle smile on her way out of the room.

I try to get sit up but the straps are on tight. I try my best to wriggle my arms free while listening for the door. My skin scratches against the straps during my struggle. I feel them starting to get sore, imagining they must be bright red by now. I try for a minute, to get my legs free but in this position, I can't even bend them to get any momentum.

The handle of the door creaks and I fall still.

'Hello, my name is Dr Leeson. I've been asked to examine your injuries. Where are you getting the pain from?'

He is short and bald with thin glasses and a weathered face.

'Mostly, my back and my left elbow,' I tell him.

He leans over me, looking down. 'OK, I'm going to ask one of the officers to come in and take the restraints off you so that I can get a look at your back.'

He goes to the door and whispers to someone outside. A policeman follows Dr Leeson back inside. The policeman comes over to my stretcher and starts to take off the straps.

'No funny business now, there's another three cops outside that door,' he tells me as he unhooks the second strap.

Once they've all been removed, I sit up and stretch my arms, trying to keep my back still in the process to keep the act going.

'Can you please remove your top?' Dr Leeson asks.

I take off my top and lay on my side with my back to the doctor.

I feel his cold hands touching spots of my back.

'Hmm, yeah I think we need to get an x-ray to be sure if there is any real damage,' he concludes.

I feel his cold hands move away so I sit up again and put my top back on.

'X-ray is overcrowded at the minute, it would be better if we wait at least an hour until it empties out a little bit. This room should be available to you for the rest of this evening should you need it. I'll send a nurse when we are ready for him,' Dr Leeson explains to the policeman.

'OK, thank you, Doctor,' the policeman says.

Dr Leeson leaves.

The policeman turns to me.

'Listen, you might as well use the bed while you're in here. We'll be right outside the door so please don't mess about,' and with that, he leaves.

I pull my feet over the edge of the stretcher and slowly lower myself down. When I put the weight down, I limp over to the bed, just in case one of the cops were to come in and see my miraculous recovery.

Slowly, carefully, I go to the window but it is locked. I hear someone brushing against the door on the other side so I get up onto the bed before easing myself down onto the mattress. It's not the most comfortable position but it will do, but no one enters.

Before long, after listening to the sounds of the hospital beyond the door and the singing of the birds on the trees outside. That is when a sound startles me, it seems like it was very close and it didn't come from the door into the room.

I know what that is, the flushing sound of a toilet. It came from my toilet. How? Is someone camped up in there? The sound of doors opening and closing follow, then silence. That makes me think, there must be another door leading out of the toilet.

I stop contemplating getting up and just do it.

I go over to the door of what I believe to be the toilet and open it. Beyond the door, I am not met with what I

94

expected at all. On the other side of the door is a small corridor with two other doors inside. One on my left and one straight ahead. Keeping in line with my act, I use the wall to take some of my weight walking to the first door on the left.

I open the door and swing it open. Inside there is the toilet. A shared toilet between two rooms. It then dawns on me that the other door is my pathway out of here. A lifeline when I needed it most. Then is hear a voice on the other side of the door.

'It's OK, I'll get a tissue from the toilet,' a man's voice says.

I freeze on the spot.

I'll just have to play on my injuries and go with the sympathy card.

The door opens ahead and the man steps into the corridor.

'Wait, what the fuck? What are you doing?' Carl asks.

Carl's confusion is in equal to my surprise at the sight of each other.

'Long story. Is Harry OK?' I ask.

'Yeah he's in here, he's OK.'

'Who that?' Harry's distant voice shouts.

'It's Michael,' Carl says back to Harry.

'Where's he been?'

'The cops are here with me,' I tell Carl.

'What?' Carl asks, giving me a look of shock.

He walks past me and gently opens my door ajar, looking in.

'Where?' he asks.

'They're outside my door.'

'What did you do?'

'I took out Chester's crew.'

'On your own?' Carl asks, surprised. 'Did you get Chester?'

'No, Willy got all country-western with his shotgun so I had to get away.'

'I see that worked out well,' Carl says sarcastically.

I give him a hand gesture and my hand slips on the wall but Carl catches me before I fall to the floor.

'C'mon, we need to get you outta here,' Carl says.

Harry's eyes fix to us when we bundle into the room. I've finally dropped the act of being hurt and I am determined to get out of here.

'Where the hell were you?' Harry asks me.

'I've got to get Michael out of here,' Carl says, going to the window.

'What happened?' Harry asks me.

I can see he is in hospital clothing, on his bed with his back against the headboard in an upright position. I open my mouth to speak, to give him an answer but Carl cuts in.

'I'll tell ya when I get back,' he says, sliding the window open.

I go over towards the window. I get up onto the window sill and carefully climb outside and look down.

We are on the first floor. It's a bit of a drop but I've seen worse.

'You're gonna have to jump. I'll be right behind ya,' Carl tells me.

I turn my head back into the room.

'How about you fuckin' go first then?' I ask sarcastically.

'Just go, we don't have time to mess about.'

I look out at the grass below, trying to judge the height by eye.

The more I think about it, the more I worry about it. I feel myself hesitating and second-guessing. I know it will be my undoing. I clear my head and throw my lead foot off the window sill, my other foot follows with the momentum and I crash down onto the grass below.

My feet make contact first, followed rapidly by my knees and then my left shoulder which takes the brunt of the fall. I wince at the pain but it goes away moments later when I climb onto my feet. I look up and watch as Carl drops from the window above.

He lands on the grass and lands on his feet but is unable to absorb the impact and ends up on his back. Looking around, he then scrambles to his feet, grabs me around the shoulders and ushers me through the hospital grounds. We make our way around to the front of the hospital, following the small roads leading up to it.

Taxis drive past and Carl tries to flag them down but none of them stop. There are a lot of people at the front of the hospital, as soon as one taxi leaves, five arrive. It's a constant hotbed of activity.

'We'll get you a taxi OK? Go back to my flat and wait for me there,' Carl tells me before he tries to signal down another taxi with no luck.

We reach the front entrance of the hospital where Carl leaves me to go down the line of parked taxis, hoping to get one of them to take me.

I slump onto one of the metal benches scattered beside the entrance, the relief of taking the weight off my feet is temporary when my back hits the cold metal of the bench. I take a moment to take in my surroundings.

Carl goes from taxi window to taxi window, bargaining. People from all walks of life and all ages go back and forth in front of my feet. Some with visible smiles, others distressed while the vast majority show no signs at all.

The cold, wet speckles of rain start to drop on my hands between my legs. A slight wind starts to blow it into the side of my face when I hear Carl's voice shout for me.

I get up and walk down the line of taxis to the one that Carl is standing beside.

'OK, get in. I'll meet you at the flat tonight. Just stay low.'

Carl pulls a key from his pocket and gives it to me. He gives the address to the driver before shutting my door.

On the drive to Carl's apartment, I can't help but notice a blue car that seems to be going the same way as us.

I start to get the suspicion that I am being followed. I tell the taxi driver to take a diversion to a small shop.

Once we are parked outside the shop, I notice the blue car continuing on the main road. I go on in to the shop anyway and get myself a drink and a microwaveable burger. I come back out again, immediately checking for signs of the blue car before getting back into the taxi.

The taxi finally leaves me off outside Carl's apartment block and I pay the fare. Opening my door to get out, the blue car slowly drives past, parking a little further down the street.

I pause, halfway of getting out of the taxi.

What if this is some sort of ambush?

I check my pocket to feel Carl's key.

'What are ya doing'? Ya getting out or what?' the taxi driver asks angrily.

With nowhere else to go, I'm taking my chances. Getting out of the taxi, I rush to the doors of the apartment block, trying to make it seem casual instead of panicked. I climb the stairs to the fourth floor and open up number "41" as marked on the key fob.

The smell of damp hits my senses when I close the door behind me. The floorboards are exposed with stains and scratched the whole way along them.

I go into the kitchen and find a roll of bin liners in the cupboards. I take two and go back to the ground floor, to the bin outside. I'm careful not to catch the eyes of anyone as I raid the bin for my packages of cocaine. I also search to the bottom to find the Glock and the rifle I stashed too. I stuff them all inside my bin liners and take them back to the apartment.

I hide them in Carl's room, under his bed.

I go to the living room and look out of the closed curtains to the road below. The car is still there, smoke, which I assume is from a cigarette, flows out of the open window.

My brother mustn't have many people around, even the sofa is ripped. The floor has been used as an ashtray, I'm almost frightened to see the state of the kitchen. I go and swap out my ripped t-shirt for one of Carl's from his room. I come back into the living room and fall onto the ripped sofa in the dying light of the day.

DAY FIVE

A noise startles me awake, I think I hear faint knocking. I freeze to listen, there's no way it came from the door. Then I hear it again, it is coming from the door.

I check the time on my phone, it's nine in the morning.

I've slept through the entire night.

Does Carl not have a spare key?

I sneak into the hall, carefully treading, trying to avoid finding any creaking floorboards. To my relief, the pain in my back has gone. Another series of knocks come when I get into the hall.

'Carl are you gonna answer the door or what?' a woman's voice shouts.

I open the door to a short, beautiful blonde woman, she must be in her mid-twenties.

'Hey, who are you?' she asks.

'I'm Michael, I'm Carl's brother.'

'Is Carl here?'

'He should be back soon, you want me to get him to call you?'

'It's OK, I'll wait,' she says, casually walking past me into the apartment.

I shut the door again and follow her into the living room.

'He's an absolute pig your brother,' she says, moving a pile of junk mail off the sofa and onto the floor.

She then pulls out a packet of cigarettes and lights one up. She takes her first draw before offering the packet out to me.

'You smoke?' she asks.

I take one out of the packet and get a light from her.

'Thanks,' I say, going to the window and opening it.

'I'm Naomi by the way,' she says, flicking her ash on the floor.

'Naomi Spencer? From school?' I ask, recognising her face.

'Oh, you remember me?' she asks, smiling.

'Yeah, you used to run about with Ryan's crowd.'

'Yeah, that's a while back.'

'So, you and Carl a thing?'

'We met up last summer when he came back from a tour. Since then we've been meeting up as much as we can when he is home,' she tells me, blushing.

'He shouldn't be too long,' I say, blowing my cigarette smoke out of the open window. I hope he is back soon. I need him.

'How about you? You got yourself someone these days?' Naomi asks.

'Yeah,' I say hesitantly.

'Well?' she asks, probing for more information. 'What's she like?' she asks, stubbing out her cigarette on the floor under one of her knee-high boots.

'She's great, her name is Lisa. We're married actually.'

'Wow, really?' her voice getting excited. 'How long?'

'Two years. We have a little girl too.'

'Aww, what age is she?'

'She's five, Layla,' I tell her, forcing a smile.

'That's lovely, go you!'

102

'Thanks. Hope ya don't mind but I haven't had much sleep,' I lie, I just find this incredibly awkward.

'No, no, don't worry go ahead,' Naomi says smiling.

'Like I said, Carl shouldn't be long. I'm sure he will be glad to see you.'

'I hope so. I'll see you later maybe,' she says.

I toss my finished cigarette out of the window and I leave her in the living room and go to the bedroom.

I try to call Carl but he doesn't answer. I send him a text explaining that Naomi is here and that we need to get moving with the plan.

I lay on the bed in silence, wanting to avoid Naomi and waiting for Carl to get back.

I'm wasting time but I can't go ahead without Carl and his contacts.

***

I start to drift off to sleep until I hear the sound of voices piercing the walls.

I can hear Carl's voice, he's back.

I listen in to his conversation with Naomi.

'You really can't be here right now,' I hear Carl say.

'Why have you been ignoring all of my calls? You think I don't know what's going on? Everyone is looking for your brother! What happened to his little girl?'

'She got taken by Michael's old gang, that's all I can tell you,' Carl tells her.

'Listen, me and you, let's just go. We've been talking about it for ages, I've saved the money, we can finally get away,' Naomi pleads.

'I'm not leaving my brother like this. He's family and so is Layla, she's my niece.'

I pick my moment to get out of bed and stumble into the living room in a break of their conversation.

'Hey, everything OK?' I ask, playing dumb.

Their faces are both intense and serious, Naomi's mouth slightly ajar as if she were about to unleash a barrage of words, but they don't come.

'Yeah, everything is fine,' Carl says in a dismissive tone, breaking the silence.

'How about Harry?'

'He's still in the hospital. He's asleep so I thought I would pop back here to relax for a bit,' Carl says.

'The real reason I'm here is, I need a place to stay for tonight,' Naomi admits to Carl.

'You're always free to stay here whenever you want. Your dad kicking up again?'

'You know what he's like after a couple of drinks. It's passed on from the nights, now he's starting during the day.'

'However long you need,' Carl tells her.

'Thanks,' Naomi says with a slight smile. She disappears into the kitchen where the rising of the kettle is followed.

'Hey,' I whisper to Carl.

'What?' he snaps back in a whisper.

'Can we trust her?'

'Don't worry about her,' he snaps defencelessly.

'OK, I'm just asking because we have cops and a mob after us, plus the fact we need to reel in thousands from drug money,' I tell him in a sarcastic tone.

'I'll deal with her, she's OK. You don't need to worry.'

Naomi returns from the kitchen with a cup of tea.

'Everything OK?' she asks.

'Yeah, good,' Carl lies.

I sit, mostly in silence throughout the small talk exchanged between Carl and Naomi. I nip out of the room to the exile of the kitchen every now and then for a quick break to maintain my sanity from their normal conversation.

Nothing feels normal to me lately, there's always that elephant in the room.

I return to the living room once again, after what is my fourth coffee in two hours. I sit down just as Carl stands up. He takes out his phone and answers a call. 'Hello? Yes...Yeah, I'm on my way. Tell him I'll be there in ten minutes. OK, thank you.'

'Who was that?' I ask swiftly.

'The hospital, they're letting Harry go home.'

'Are you bringing him back here?' Naomi asks.

'No, I'm gonna bring him back to his own house. Saying that, I need to ring my Aunt Rosie to let her know we are coming,' Carl says.

He disappears into the hall, leaving me and Naomi alone in an awkward silence. Carl pops his head into the living room after the short phone call.

'OK, that's me going now. Shouldn't take longer than an hour.'

'That's OK,' says Naomi.

I give him a quick nod and then he leaves the apartment.

Me and Naomi sit for another five minutes before she breaks the silence.

'How are you holding up?' she asks.

'Fine,' I say, understanding what she is getting at.

'I know it must be hard. Poor little girl's photograph is all over the news and the papers.'

105

Exactly the conversation I wanted to avoid, especially with a basic stranger. Naomi may be sleeping with Carl but I haven't spoken to her since we left school. I'm a completely different person now, we don't know each other at all, but still, the conversation goes on even though I try to stop it dead.

'Yeah well, posting up missing posters wasn't going to do anything,' I say sarcastically.

'What about the police? They're looking.'

'I'm sorry but you wouldn't understand, you never ran with these people. The cops aren't going to do shit, some of them have their pockets filled by these men.'

'So you're going to be the difference?'

'I'm her only chance, me and Carl.'

She looks away and starts to fidget with her hands at the mention of Carl's name. I forgot that I'm inadvertently putting her boyfriend in harm's way.

I go to the window and look out. I see it as an excuse to stop talking, pretending to take an interest in our surroundings.

'I want to help you,' she says quietly.

'I don't want to drag you into this. Carl would kill me,' I tell her.

It's true though, she would be getting involved in a world she has no place in. Carl wouldn't have it for a second. Deep down, I appreciate her extending her hand but she's really of no use to us.

I keep staring out the window in a sort of daydream. My eyes start to tilt down, down until I'm looking at the road below and spotting the same blue car parked outside from when I arrived last night. There's someone inside. I can see them resting their elbow on the door of the car with the window down.

106

I get lost in my gaze until Naomi joins me at my side, looking down at the car.

'That guy has been waiting there for a long time now. He was there when I got here,' she says.

'Yeah,' I say dismissively, trying not to make a deal out of it with her.

'You think he's watching you?' she asks.

I walk away from the window and sit down.

'Well? Kind of odd don't you think?' she continues.

'Just leave it,' I say.

Naomi starts to march past me. 'If you're just gonna sit on your ass, I guess I'll go find out.'

I hear the apartment door slam shut.

'Oh for fuck's sake!' I mutter to myself, scrambling to my feet to get after her.

I get out to the staircase, I hear the echo of her shoes, already a good head-start down the stairs, she must be running. I start running after her.

I slowly gain ground on her, we both get to the ground floor around the same time. She opens the front door of the block but I push it shut again.

'What the hell are you doing?' I ask, breathing heavily from chasing.

'You wanna find out what he's up to? Here's your chance. I'll distract him.'

'No, no way, you're not getting to be bait.'

'It's not up to you, one way or another, I'm going out that door,' she says, pointing.

I grab her lightly by the arm and start dragging her back to the stairs.

'We're not doing this. We're going upstairs to wait for Carl.'

107

'Let go of me!' she shouts, struggling.

I get her right over at the start of the steps when she catches me by surprise and kicks me really hard in the shin. I let go of her, clutching my leg and look up to see her running out the door. I limp over to the door.

I watch Naomi walk over to the car from behind the glass window of the door. She leans her head in the open window of the driver's side door and sparks up a conversation with the guy inside.

I ease open the apartment block door and creep along the edge of the building and use a couple of parked cars for cover.

I keep my eyes on them, the driver has no interest in me which tells me I haven't been spotted yet. I cross the road and duck behind the row of cars. I slowly move up along them, one by one, keeping low until I see the blue shell of the target car. I close enough to listen in to their conversation.

That's when I recognise that voice.

I know it from somewhere but I can't pin it down.

I rise, looking through the windows of the last car I'm hiding behind. I see through the windscreen of the car spotting Naomi talking to the man. That's why I recognise the voice, I'd have never of guessed it to be Andy, the mechanic.

I stay low, walking right under the passenger door window. I slowly rise up, his focus still on Naomi.

I open the passenger door and reach in to grab Andy. He spots me and shoves open his door, knocking Naomi to the ground before running up the street. I chase after him.

108

I run hard and fast after his large frame, determined. He must have been the one who led Tommy to me. To my house, to Layla.

The building rage mixed with the adrenaline makes me close down the distance quickly. I'm right up behind him on the footpath. I shoot my hand out and grab the hood of his jumper and yank it backwards.

The power of the pull drags Andy back, off his feet and crashing to the ground. A sickening thud of his skull smacking the concrete makes me wince momentarily. I place my knee on his chest to stop him from going anywhere but it then becomes evident that it isn't necessary as he isn't moving and his eyes are shut.

'Andy!' I shout at him, slapping his face and trying to wake him up.

'Andy, where are they? Where are they?' I continue.

Naomi catches up to us.

I cradle the back of Andy's head.

'Andy!' I shout again as I bring his face closer to my own. Then I freeze.

I slowly lower his head back to the pavement and draw my hand out. It's covered in blood.

'What's wrong?' Naomi asks, worryingly.

'Help me get him inside,' I ask.

I get his arms and shoulders while Naomi lifts his legs. We start carrying him back up the street when a worried neighbour rushes down from his garden to us.

'Hey, he OK?' the neighbour asks.

'Yeah, he's my cousin, took a bad fall,' I lie.

'Do you want me to call an ambulance?'

'No, it's fine, gonna take him inside. If he gets worse I'll take him to the hospital myself,' I tell him.

The man gives me the thumbs up and goes back inside. Me and Naomi struggle with Andy back up into the apartment.

'Get one of the kitchen chairs,' I tell Naomi once we set Andy down in the hallway of Carl's apartment. She comes back with the chair and I hoist Andy up onto it.

'Hold him up for a sec,' I tell Naomi.

I go off to the kitchen to raid the cupboards for something to bind him with. The drawers are mostly empty, just tiny bits of junk here and there, like batteries and cables.

I continue my search in Carl's bedroom when an idea comes to me. Going to the bottom of the wardrobe, I strip the laces out of an old pair of shoes.

When I come back into the hall, I pull Andy's arms behind the chair and tie them tightly using the shoelaces. I grab the sides of the chair from behind and start to drag it.

'Let him go,' I tell Naomi. She stops pressing Andy against the chair and he slumps forward until his bounded arms stop him from falling off.

I drag him and the chair back into the kitchen. I struggle to get the chair over a small lip on the floor at the kitchen doorway where the floor level changes. The weight of the chair is heavier than I expected when I attempt to lift it over the lip.

Andy has always been a big guy but even at that, I thought this would be an easy task. After a minute, mixed feelings of frustration and anger start to kick in.

I start jiggling the chair side to side, banging it against the door frame, trying to lift at least one of the chair legs over but it doesn't work. I've had enough. I can see in Naomi's face as she watches on, she is beginning to scare. I

110

walk around to the front of Andy and kick him hard in the chest. It sends him and the chair crashing onto their backs.

I turn to say something to Naomi. Maybe it was something comforting, something to tell her to not be afraid, but it's disappeared from thought now. I leave her in the hallway, walking into the kitchen and shutting the door.

I pick Andy back up off the floor I pull up my own chair next to him and patiently wait for him to wake up.

There's no movement from him at all.

After a few minutes, I fill a cup of water and throw it in his face, no reaction. I even slap him about a little, hoping it will help but it doesn't. I'm starting to think that knock to the head has done some serious damage.

I go through the last of Carl's sugar in making myself a coffee, then I hear coughing. I put the cup of coffee down and rush over to Andy, he is still slumped over in his seat. I kneel down to look at his face but his eyes are still wide shut.

Am I starting to imagine things?

He coughs again even louder and I'm in the best spot to catch him in the act. I lightly slap his cheeks.

'Hey! Hey! Andy!' I call.

He raises his head slightly to look at me through glazed eyes.

'What were you doing outside?'

'What? What are you talking about?' he asks groggily.

'You've been parked outside watching my brother's apartment, are you spying on us?'

'Michael, please, let me go,' his voice not sounding any better. I can hear the pain and tiredness in it.

'I'll let you go if you tell me what you've been doing Andy.'

He doesn't answer, he starts swaying slightly in his seat before finding a little strength to straighten up and adjust himself in the seat, that's when he notices that his hands are tied.

'Tell me where she is and I'll let you go, I swear it,' I threaten.

'I can't, they'll kill me,' he says.

'They'll kill you? Who will kill you?'

'I can't say.'

'Tommy? Tommy's crew will kill you?'

'It's in both of our interests if you let me go right now,' he says, regaining his fluidity of speech, free of grogginess and slurring.

'Why is that?' I ask.

'If you want to get her back you need to let me go and I'll never mention a word of this.'

'Oh, wait, you think you're in control here?' I ask, outraged at his arrogance.

'If you want Layla back—'

I punch him in the chest, winding him, not letting him finish the sentence.

'Don't even fucking dare say her name!' I tell him in a scathing tone.

The gravity of this revelation then dawns on me. This is how Tommy found me.

'You're the one who told Tommy where to find me.'

'My cousin knows his crowd down south. I heard your name pop up and mentioned it to my cousin. He told me I could earn what they call a finder's fee. The garage isn't doing great, I have two mortgages to pay for—'

'I don't give a fuck what you have to pay for!' I shout. 'My house, my family...my five-year-old little girl!'

My fists don't need my guidance in finding their target now that I'm over the breaking point. I lay out on Andy, strike, after strike, until my muscles burn and I stop, catching my breath.

Andy starts to cough and wince from the beating. I keep all of my shots low, avoiding his face as I plan to use him.

'If you help me I'll let you live, I promise you that right now. Otherwise, I'll put a bullet in your head. Why were you waiting for us outside?' I ask under heavy breaths.

Andy defiantly spits on the kitchen floor but then submits.

'After I made the call, Tommy wanted me to follow you. Watch over you to make sure you get the money and not get caught by the cops or try any funny shit.'

'You get paid extra for that?' I ask sarcastically.

'We know, he knows what you guys have been doing. The whole drug fiasco with that English fella.'

'Does he know how much we lost today?'

'Not yet, I'm guessing you want to keep that a secret?'

'What about my little girl? What about Layla?' I ask, my voice becoming desperate.

'I don't know much about her.'

'Do you know if she's safe right now? Do you know where they are keeping her?'

'I don't know where she is but I know that she's alive.'

'How do you fill them in with what me and Carl are up to?'

He turns away, looking around the kitchen not wanting to answer.

'How?' I ask more insistently.

'He's got a guy in Belfast that I meet every day at two o'clock. Name is Barry. Always the same coffee shop. Would be easier to just give the guy a phone call but he's really old school. He's the paranoid type as well, thinks that all calls are tapped and the cops on the other end listening.'

'Where is the coffee shop?'

'It's on the Lisburn road.'

I check the time on my phone.

'One o'Clock, we've got an hour. You're going to be on time today, I'll be coming with you. If you let anything slip, I'll give you that bullet I promised you.'

I hear the front door of the apartment open and slam shut.

The faint sound of Naomi crying is soon drowned out by indistinct talking.

It is followed by the kitchen door swinging open, revealing Carl standing there.

'What the fuck is going on?' he asks.

'He's been spying on us from the very start,' I say.

'Andy?' Carl says, recognizing Andy through the blood and bruises.

'He's the one that led Tommy to me.'

Carl settles down and straightens up.

'What are we gonna do with him then?' he asks.

'He's got a contact here in Belfast. I'm going along with him to meet now.'

'Well, I'm coming with you,' Carl says.

'No, I need you to start collecting today. The money needs to start rolling in. We need to get a straight-out price for what we have left, it's hidden under your bed.'

'You hid it under my bed?' Carl asks surprised.

I untie Andy and lift him to his feet.

'There is a Glock and a rifle in the bag too if you need them,' I tell Carl.

I march Andy to the bathroom to clean the blood out of what remains of his hair.

I then walk him out of the apartment, down the flight of stairs and out onto the street.

I hand him the keys as we approach his car.

'You drive, you know where it is.'

We get in and start driving.

***

We arrive at the coffee shop with half an hour to spare.

I instruct Andy to park further down the road in the fear of being seen with him.

I get out of the car and walk down to the coffee shop, leaving Andy behind to wait until the designated time. I order a large latte and take a seat at the back of the café where most of the shoppers have congregated, hiding myself amongst them.

I take my time sipping on the coffee, knowing how long I have to make it last. I take a newspaper from the rack on the wall. It's two days old but it doesn't bother me, it's just for show.

The illusion of blending in, it also helps to keep my mind occupied instead of the alternative which would be counting the lines in the small, round wooden table I am sat at.

The time approaches five to two. I see Andy entering the café and order a coffee over the top of my newspaper. He casually looks around as he waits, my mind wonders whether he is looking for me or the man he knows as Barry.

With his coffee in hand, he finds a seat close to the window and sits alone.

Another ten minutes roll past, I've exhausted all of the interesting articles of the newspaper and have begun reading the agony aunt's section about people's affairs and addiction to porn. I start to bring into question Barry's punctuation, is he always late? Does he know something is up? Has Andy tipped him off? I resist the urge to approach Andy to lay on my questions and instead, I wait.

My patience pays off as just as I finish reading the last word on the page, a man takes a seat opposite Andy. He is a large man like Andy, with a close shaved head, sporting a tracksuit top with sweat bottoms.

I have to time this perfectly. One false move at the wrong moment and I could fuck it all up. I let them sit in conversation against my best judgement, I don't trust Andy not to tell Barry that I am here but I've no choice. I can't tackle him in a crowded café. I sit watching them talking, knowing that I'm vulnerable to being exposed at every rally of speech.

I'm desperate to hear what they are saying and wish everyone else in the café would just shut up. I try my best not to stare at them for too long or, at worst, make eye contact. I'm nearing the bottom of my cup of coffee when I notice Barry get up out of his seat. He starts to walk through the café towards me.

I look up when his eyes divert to the menu above the counter. I use the opportunity to look across at Andy for any indication of what's going on but he just looks back at me with an expressionless face. I bow my head down, looking at the newspaper on my table, pretending to read it as Barry gets closer. I hang on to the hope that he doesn't know I'm here and won't pay any attention to me, but why is he walking this way?

This is the back of the café, other than me, what's his reason to come own here?

I roll my hands into fists under the table, ready for a fight. He gets right up next to me, there is no hiding now, I look up. My eyes come off the table to look for Barry's large frame standing over me, but he's not there. I hear the slam of a door next to my table, he's just gone through it.

Looking at the door, I notice a sign, a sign that I hadn't even known was there. Maybe I should have paid more attention to it when I took a seat, it's the toilets. I hadn't known they were there as no one has used them since I sat down.

The relief is comforting, I look back over to Andy, knowing my trust was not misplaced. Now Barry has walked right into the perfect scenario for me, he's cornered himself, not out of an elaborate, thought-out trap, but by pure chance.

I dare not waste the opportunity or any time, I get up out of my seat and go into the toilets.

Once I pass through the door, I'm greeted by three more in a small hallway, I take the door on the right, which is the male toilets.

I expect to find Barry stood at the urinals but that would've been too easy. The toilets are completely empty, as I knew they would be. I walk carefully around the front of the cubicles to find the one that has the door shut and locked. Now it's a waiting game.

I walk over to the urinals, I take a spot in the corner so no one can see that I am faking it. I just stand there to wait. Then things get more complicated, two men walk into the toilets and take a spot at the urinals, laughing and joking between themselves.

I hear the cubicle door opening behind me, I see the movement of the door in a reflection of the metallic urinal wall. I sneak a peek, peering past the two men and spotting Barry at the sink washing his hands.

The two men act like a brick wall between me and my target. The opportunity is gone, but I have the compulsion I needed to act, I can't let him just slip from my grasp so easily.

He leaves the men's room and I chase after him just before the door closes behind him. I meet him in the small hallway, his back is to me.

I grab him from behind around the neck and drag him into the disabled toilet off to the right. We crash to the floor and I kick closed the door using my feet. Barry struggles, he's very strong and I almost lose my grip.

He gets to his knees and then to his feet, with me still hanging on. He slams me into the wall, narrowly avoiding the white handle to help people down onto the toilet. He slams me into the wall again, I lose hold of him. He starts to punch me, I cover my face with my hand and he starts aiming for my body. A strong punch winds me which slumps me momentarily. He grabs my throat, squeezing and pushing my neck against the wall behind me.

I feel my Adam's apple being pushed to the back of my throat. Choking but unable to cough or even breathe, my eyes start to strain and water from the pressure. I don't care about fighting fairly, it's survival now. I kick him, as hard as I can, in the nuts.

He releases my throat and drops to the ground in pain, holding the spot I kicked. I don't give him any chance, I start punching him in the face, imagining he was Tommy. I

118

don't beat him up too badly, just bad enough so he can't fight back or escape.

I lock the toilet door and then walk back towards Barry laying on the floor, ready to fire my questions. I get down on my knees beside him and grip him by the collar.

'Where is my daughter?'

'I don't know,' Barry slurs back.

I shake him by his collar. 'Where is she?'

'I don't know where they are keeping her.'

'Yeah? You sure about that?'

I punch him in the nuts with my free hand, adding to his pain. He wriggles around in pain from the shot but I keep hold of his collar, controlling him.

'Where is she?' I shout, fed up of his games.

It takes a minute for him to settle down enough to answer, and even when he does, it's under heavy breaths.

'They didn't tell me where she is. The only way you will get your daughter back is if you pay the money!' he shouts.

I look around to check the door, he shouted so loud someone must've heard. I'm expecting someone to try the door handle any second, but to my relief, it doesn't happen.

Everything falls silent apart from the moans of Barry, I can't hear anyone on the other side of the door, just distant chatter and the hustle and bustle from the café.

I grab Barry's head with both hands and lean in.
'If I pay the money, is he going to let her go?' I ask, my voice becoming quiet and calm.

'You pay the money and he will let her go. I just don't know about you,' he admits.

I stand up, leaving Barry to curl up on the floor. I leave the toilet and go back into the café.

I stride straight over to Andy and hoist him up out of his seat by his arm.

'C'mon, let's go,' I say forcefully.

We leave the café and get back into the car parked up the street.

***

I start driving back to Carl's apartment, unsure of what to do with Andy. I can't just drop him off, I still see him as a threat. What if Tommy's guys catch up to him?

'Where are we going?' he asks.

'I'm heading back to Carl's place.'

'What about me?'

'Looks like you're coming too.'

'I'm in this till it's over then eh?'

I start to take notice of a black Mercedes behind us. I think he's been behind us since the café but I can't be sure, it might just be my paranoia.

I take a scenic route back to Carl's, trying to gauge whether we are being followed or not.

The road starts to open up a little, with almost no cars on it, the black Mercedes starts to get closer to us from behind. It swerves into the next lane and comes alongside us.

It swings in, ramming us, I grip the wheel tight, catching the wheels from veering off the road. My foot slams down on the accelerator, pulling away from the Mercedes but it quickly catches up, matching my speed. I notice a set of traffic lights ahead and brake sharply, turning into a side street to avoid them, the Mercedes follows.

We speed down a narrow road with cars parked either side, narrowly avoiding taking off numerous wing mirrors. Another sharp, brake turn and we come out onto another main road. I pick up the speed again quickly, seeing the Mercedes come blazing out of the narrow street behind us in the rearview mirror.

They catch up to us as we enter a large roundabout. The Mercedes slams into the side of us as we turn round the roundabout and both our cars lock into a skid. I pull out of it, coming out on the second exit but I lose control of the car and it under-steers into a traffic island.

We hit the island, taking out a traffic island bollard, and the car flips onto its roof. My seatbelt keeps me strapped in but Andy falls out onto the roof with red hot sparks dancing all around as the momentum of the crash slides us for a duration.

The car finally comes to a stop, the hot smell of metal fills my nose and the smoke from the roof burns my eyes.

I try to undo my belt but it won't click out. I feel Andy's hand's shove mine out of the way as he tries to undo the belt. A cold, wet patch irritates my thigh.

Looking down, I can see a blood-soaked spot on my jeans, but it's not from me. Andy's hands are badly cut, and as he struggles with the belt, he brushed my leg with his bloody hands.

The next thing I feel on my leg is Andy's jaw as he slips and falls. He cries out from the pain of it but then I see the source of his fall.

Two hands are wrapped around one of his legs, trying to drag him out of the car. I quickly drop my hands down to grab his, he grips back.

Holding on for his life.

'C'mon, get his other leg!' I hear a man shout from outside the car.

Another pair of hands grab Andy's other leg and my strength isn't great enough to hold on.

'I'm sorry Michael! I'm sorry!' he apologizes, on the brink of tears.

'Andy!' I shout before he is pulled from my grasp.

I watch Andy disappear from the car and then his whimpers and pleas for mercy, but he is offered none, just two bullets that ring out, I know I am next.

My car door opens and numerous hands start grabbing me, trying to pull me from the car before they notice the seat belt situation.

One of them produces a knife which cuts through my seat belt and I am dragged out of the car to see the carnage on the road. The traffic island bollard is completely destroyed with debris and contents of Andy's car lay scattered in our wake.

I'm dragged away from the wreckage.

For me, surprisingly there is no bullet, just a car ride in the boot of the Mercedes.

The lid shuts down on top of me once I'm thrown inside, leaving me in darkness with little space to move.

***

When the boot opens again, I'm blinded by the light, and it's not a particularly bright day either. It takes my eyes a moment to adjust, I'm still trying to focus when they drag me out.

My knees fall onto the road, it takes me a minute to find my feet in this dazed state whilst being escorted along a series of rusted rental garages.

I see one of them with the shutter open, I assume that is where we are headed.

Once we are inside, the shutter is pulled down, sending the garage into darkness before the dim overhead lights come on.

The men tie me to an unstable wooden chair, I feel it rocking as they bind my hands and legs to its fragile frame with cable ties, one of the legs must be uneven. It seems ironic that just over an hour ago, I was playing the reversed role on Andy, binding him to a chair.

Once my arms and legs are tied, the men disappear into the darkness at the edge of the room. I try blinking to get rid of the blur in my vision but it only gets worse, now being accompanied by a straining headache and a ringing in my ears.

That's when I hear footsteps approaching.

A man walks around the front of me.

All I notice at first is his cleanly polished black shoes, above them are formal black trousers and as my eyes draw up his suit, I see the man inside it, Chester.

Then I put it all together and why I am still alive.

'You've got balls, my friend. Big massive balls. You nearly succeeded too, and all by yourself, a one-man army,' he says in a calculated voice.

'Thanks, wanna see them?' I antagonise, I know I'm screwed.

'No, thank you. But what I do want to see is my product. Would you be able to tell me where the rest is? I noticed some was missing.'

123

I keep my mouth shut.

He outstretches his arm, gesturing to one of his men who brings him a chair.

He puts it alongside mine and takes a seat, talking closely into my ear.

'You know, we have ways of making people sing, this isn't the first time I've encountered a selective mute,' he says, threateningly.

The shutter opens again and another man is escorted in by Chester's men.

'Strap him in and put him next to this one,' Chester insists.

They do the same to the other man as they did to me, once tied to the chair they drag him over next to me, it's Andy, he's alive.

'Now we are going to play a little game, a quiz game with a difference, Willy...'

Willy appears with a black baton, he hands it over to Chester.

'Everyone else out!' Chester shouts.

Chester's men leave the garage, closing the shutter, but not fully, behind them.

'Question number one, where is the coke?' Chester asks me, pointing the baton at me.

I shake my head at him.

He winds up the baton and swings it into my shin, the pain is excruciating, I can't contain the scream I let out. I writhe in the chair, trying to subside the pain as Chester hands over the baton to Willy who is stood in front of Andy.

'Question number one, again. Where is the coke?' Willy asks Andy, a distinctive glee in his voice.

124

'What coke? I have nothing to do with this.'

Willy swings the baton into one of Andy's bound arms, I'm almost certain I hear it break. Andy screams out louder than I did.

Willy hands the baton back over to Chester, my turn again.

I see where this is going.

'Question number one. Where is the coke?' Chester asks more aggressively this time.

I give him no answer again.

He swings the baton at the same leg again with all his strength, before I even have time to react, he swings down for a second time. I writhe around and nearly topple over from the pain.

Chester throws the baton to the ground.

'OK, let's try out the new toy,' Chester says to Willy who goes off out of sight.

I only dread to think of what this toy might be. He comes back with something small in his hand, at first I think it is a gun but then it turns out to be a taser.

'You try it first,' Chester says to Willy.

Willy approaches Andy.

'Still not want to talk?' he asks.

'I don't know where it is!' Andy cries.

Willy puts the taser to Andy's neck, I hear the humming of the electricity and Andy's body starts to shake violently. Willy takes the taser away but Andy continues to shake. In the middle of it all, Andy throws up on himself, all down his torso.

'Quick, get him off the chair, I don't want him dying just yet!' Chester shouts to Willy.

Willy undoes Andy's restraints and tips him out of the chair, onto the floor where he slowly calms down from the shakes. He lays motionless but breathing.

'OK, guess we know now to stay away from the neck,' Chester laughs and jokes as Willy hands over the taser.

'OK buddy, you know the score by now. I can't promise you'll walk out of here but if you tell me, it will be painless,' Chester tells me.

'Suck the back of them,' I tell him.

He pokes the taser into my chest, it's like an ice-cold shock at first and then it quickly switches to a burning heat, like my blood is boiling.

The shaking is unavoidable, it's a reaction you can't control.

I'm starting to miss the baton.

He takes it away and I finally get a chance to get a breath. I can't take that sort of punishment numerous times.

Chester hands the taser back over to Willy before he takes off his blazer, walking around trying to find somewhere to hang it.

The one thing I paid most attention to during the shock was that the wooden frame by my right arm had split during my struggle.

'Straining work, don't want to get anything on my suit,' he tells Willy.

Willy leans over Andy who is laid on his side on the floor. 'Hey, hey, gonna wake up yet eh?' he plays.

Willy turns to shout at Chester who has hung his blazer over a far off table, now walking back rolling up his sleeves.

'What are we gonna do with this one?' Willy asks.

I see Andy's eyes open.

126

He reaches up, grabbing the hand of Willy with the taser in it and forces it into Willy's head. The humming sound comes back and Willy's body shakes violently, he drops motionless to the floor.

Andy starts to get up to find his feet, just as he gets one foot up, Chester tackles him. Andy gets a hold of Chester and they start wrestling on the ground.

I start tugging my right arm, splitting the wooden frame even more.

I break that part of the chair and get my arm free.

Checking on Andy, they both still have a hold of each other.

I lean back in my chair lifting the front legs where my own legs are tied. I fight to straighten my legs one at a time, sliding the cable tie at my ankles down and off the end of the table leg, freeing myself.

One last check on Andy, Chester is on top of him, getting the better of the battle of strength. I turn my body around to free my left arm. I pull on it before resorting to striking the wooden frame, hoping to break it like the other side with a punch or an elbow. It eventually cracks and then snaps. I pull my arm free.

I run up and knee Chester in the face before he finds his feet.

He falls to the ground cradling his head, I take the chance to pick up the taser and help Andy to his feet.

As I pull Andy up, my legs give way but he catches me.

My body has just remembered the baton shots I took to the leg, it becomes fragile.

'Here, get him up,' I tell Andy, handing him the taser.

Andy picks Chester up off the floor, holding the taser to the back of his head, he walks him back over to me.

'We're gonna use him to get outta here. Give me the taser,' I say.

I grab Chester by the shoulder with one hand and hold the taser to him with the other. I use him for balance as well as a shield. We go to the shutter and press it, hiding behind the cover of Chester.

The shutter opens and we see two of his men right outside.

'Drop the guns!' I shout at them, holding the taser to the side of Chester's head for them to see.

They do as they are told, I walk Chester forward, Andy stays behind me. I see the rest of his men two shutters up. They spot us and start walking slowly down on us.

'Throw your guns on the roof!' I shout at the two men in front of us.

They slowly pick up the guns they just dropped and throw them over our heads onto the garage roof.

'Go!' I shout to Andy.

He starts running, I give him a quick head start.

The rest of Chester's men start to get close.

I push Chester into the two men ahead and run to catch up with Andy.

We come out of the garage grounds into a housing estate with lots of trees.

I stumble, falling under my own weight onto the road.

Andy stops ahead of me and notices me fall.

He runs back, picks me up and throws my arm over his shoulder, dragging me up the street on my feet.

We run through the streets, zig-zagging in our choice of turns. My run is more like an extremely fast limp.

We eventually end up in an alleyway, knowing we can't change our minds and turn now, they're right on us, we sprint towards the end.

If they catch up, we will be like fish in a barrel, even from a long way off.

I keep constantly checking over my shoulder for them the whole way down the alley.

We come upon a gate, it looks like it leads into a school or the grounds of some sort of building beyond.

The walls either side of the alley are too high to scale so we are left with no choice but to climb the gate.

Andy takes the left side of the gate and I take the other, we don't have time to take turns. I get to the top but slip at the last part of the climb. I slide down the gate and onto the ground again. My tank is running on empty. Andy jumps back off the top of the fence back down to me. He gives me a leg up, pushing me up the face of the gate to grab a hold of the top. I reach out and grab the top of the gate, hoisting myself up and throwing myself over to the other side.

Andy finds trouble in his footing in the gate, he can't quite fix his feet right.

'Andy c'mon! Put your foot there, and then there!' I call out from the other side.

I hear a loud bang then a spray of mist hits my face.

Opening my eyes after the spray, I find it is Andy's blood.

A large spot on his jumper keeps growing, a darkish colour.

He drops off the gate, landing on his feet before they give way and he lands on his knees, slumped face-first against the gate.

I creep up close to the gate.

'Run! Get your little girl back!' he tells me.

I freeze on the spot, stunned. He saved my life, he's made amends for what he's done, even if he was the cause of all of this.

I feel sympathetic in the moment, the tears slipping down from his eyes are a sight I know I will never forget.

'Michael go! Get out of here!' he shouts as bullets start to bounce off the gate.

I turn and leave him, running through the grounds of a school.

I run to the other side of the grounds, around the other side of the school building and climb a gate back onto the streets. I keep running until I can't run any more. I hide in a gap between two cars to look back, no one is behind me,

I'm safe.

I take a moment to catch my breath and contemplate what's just happened. I finally figure out where I am too.

It's an estate close to my parents' house, about a five-minute drive away.

Using my knowledge of the area, I catch a bus to take me up towards Carl's apartment.

***

I limp off the bus and walk towards the apartment block, checking all around as I go. I'm sick of being followed. I enter the block and struggle climbing the stairs. Each step sets its own challenge as all of the running has weakened my leg even further.

I finally reach Carl's apartment door and knock.

There is no answer. I knock again, hoping he is inside because I have nowhere else to hide.

Maybe Naomi stayed behind, maybe she's still inside, but will she answer for me? I knock one more time before giving up and sitting down against the door.

I feel like sleeping, I'm so tired and hungry. I feel myself slipping off to sleep.

I straighten myself up against the door but my eyes are too heavy. I let them fall shut but focus on staying awake, listening for people on the stairs but everything is silent. Too silent, there are no distractions from sleep, which is where I end up going.

'Michael? Michael wake up!' I hear a woman's voice call.

I open my eyes to find myself laid down in front of Carl's door.

Naomi is knelt over me with her hand on my shoulder and Carl is stood behind her with a shopping bag. I get up to my feet. I feel a slight pain in my leg but it's not as bad as earlier.

I see Carl looking me up and down.

'What happened? Where's Andy?'

I push past Carl and look down the staircase, no one is there. I look out the glass window of the staircase, no suspicious cars outside, we're clear.

'Michael?' Carl asks, worryingly.

'Let's get inside, I'll tell you everything then,' I say.

We all go inside the apartment.

Me and Carl take a seat in the living room where I explain to him everything that had happened. Naomi puts the groceries away and comes in to hear the end of my story with sandwiches they bought while they were out. It takes me no time in having two of them on my own.

Carl brings a bag into the living room and opens it for me to see inside. He managed to sell all of the coke and inside is the cash he got for it.

We count it over and over again.

We keep on coming up with the same number after the fourth time together.

Fifty-six thousand. Just over half.

'Fifty-six. What are we gonna do then?' Carl asks.

'Well, we're out of time and out of ideas. We need to bulk it up to look like a hundred somehow.'

'Won't they kind of notice?'

'Well, I don't know what the fuck else to do Carl? What do you want me to do?' I shout, losing my temper.

This isn't what I had expected. I always knew we would be short after Chester's snatch and grab but I never thought it would be this bad. I thought we'd at least hit close to seventy.

We sit in silence for a moment. I don't know what is going on in Carl's mind but mine is doing back-flips, buzzing, trying to come up with something smart that won't be a clear giveaway.

'What are the majority of notes here?' I ask Carl.

'Mostly twenties, then it's fives mixed in with tens.'

'If we stack too many fives it will look like there's fuck all there. We need it to all look like twenty stacks. The bulk of it is twenties anyway right?' I ask.

'Yeah.'

'Good. We'll fish out half of the twenties and change them to fives, we'll hide the smaller notes between the piles, we'll shuffle them well like a deck of cards.'

'Banks close in half an hour, and you want me to go round?' he asks, annoyed.

'I can't really go round now, can I? When you're there, get them money straps, you know the ones to strap them into bundles like in the movies?'

'Does the bank do them?' Carl asks surprised.

132

'Yeah, should do. You'd know that if you weren't always broke,' I joke.

'Fuck off, Scarface,' he fires back.

We separate the notes out.

Fives, tens and twenties, we even find the odd fifty, must've been selling to some posh lads.

Once we have them all in their piles, we take half of the twenties and put them into a plastic bag.

Carl takes off to the bank and I try to organise the rest of the cash into bundles spread out all over the living room floor.

Carl comes back almost half an hour later. We waste no time in bulking up the piles with his extra fives and tens. We then start using the brown straps that Carl brought back from the bank, making the bundles solid and making sure when you flick through a bundle, it isn't obvious that the smaller notes are there at a quick glance.

I start to pack the bundles inside a gym bag but nothing seems to sit right to my liking. The way they sit inside the bag, laying at all angles, some of the smaller notes lay exposed. This might not work, then I have an idea. 'Carl,' I call.

'Yeah, what is it?'

'I need you to head out again.'

'For fuck's sake, why?'

'Look,' I say to him.

He comes over and looks inside the bag at the half a dozen bundles I've put inside. 'You can see it as clear as day.'

'Fuck,' he mutters, running his hand over his mouth, thinking. 'What do you need to me head out for?' he asks.

'A briefcase,' I say.

'You're joking aren't ya?'

133

'In a briefcase, all of the cash will lay flat, face up and organised. It won't flap about when we're carrying it either, less chance of anything falling loose.'

'Where am I meant to get one?'

'Try one of them catalogue shops. They're bound to have some for sale.'

'Right, OK,' He says as he goes to the door again.

'Get some food when you're out.'

'Anything else?' Carl asks sarcastically.

'Nah, that's all,' I say.

He leaves and comes back with a silver briefcase, the type that you'd see a top businessman carrying. He also has brought back fish and chips. We shuffle them down before handling the cash.

We start to place the bundles inside the deep briefcase with military precision.

Every top note has to be crisp and flat in order to hide the uneven sides, every column and every row has to be aligned, straight and level. When we are done, it's just like something out of a movie, it would fool me at first glance.

We wait for six o'clock anxiously.

I pace the room, looking at my phone in my hand, waiting for it to light up. Carl sits with his eyes fixed on the closed briefcase. Everything is set.

We are dressed, coats hung over the sofa, ready to lift. Carl mentions to me that he filled Naomi's car full of petrol when he got the fish and chips, we are ready to go on a seconds notice.

The call finally comes. I answer it nervously.

'Hello?'

'There's a festival down in Drogheda this week. They've set up some sort of carnival down there in a large field. I

134

trust you'll find it. Get your ass down and go to the big tent. They've cornered it off for the week. Some poor bastard got bit by one of them big ass tigers. My mate Dean was there and saw it. Gruesome,' Tommy says.

'Make sure you bring Layla. If I can't see her when I get down there, I walk, you get absolutely nothing.'

'Shut the hell up and get in your car, boy. You're in no position to make threats. We'll see you real soon.'

Tommy hangs up.

'So what's happening?' asks Carl.

I open the briefcase again to check the tidiness of the notes.

'We're meeting them inside some carnival tent down in Drogheda.'

'Did he say where in Drogheda?'

'Nah.'

'C'mon we better get going then. It could take us ages trying to find this place,' Carl says getting up.

I close over the briefcase and lift it up.

Carl goes over and lifts up one of the large ripped cushions off the sofa.

I notice him picking something up from it before putting the cushion back down.

'What's that?'

He is in the process of stuffing whatever it is into his jeans.

'Got it from Connal, a goodwill gesture,' he says, revealing a small revolver tucked into his jeans. He then lifts his t-shirt over it and lets it drop, sheltering the handle.

At least it's something.

I go to the hallway and put my hand on the night latch of the door, ready to open it. Naomi comes out from the bedroom, meeting Carl upon leaving the living room. I put my eyes on the floor as they share their goodbyes, trying my best to block out the some-what romantic speech.

They share a kiss, then Carl starts his march to the door.

'Let's go,' he says in a no-nonsense tone, ready to go to work.

We march down the staircase, out into the street and into Naomi's car. Carl takes the driver's seat and we start the long drive to Drogheda.

***

We share little words on the drive down to the Republic of Ireland. It's only when we get on the motorway that I remember that in our rush out of the door, I forgot to pack my own guns. The Glock and the rifle are still under Carl's bed. We are going to have to rely on his revolver should anything go wrong.

We both have unflinching gazes upon the road ahead, anticipating all the outcomes of what may unfold at this carnival.

Carl chops the travel time by nearly a third by pushing the car to its limit the entire way from Belfast, barely slowing even for roundabouts. We're flying, the roar of the engine becomes like an inner voice in my head, a creature dashing to its prey.

Apart from signposts, the best giveaway that you have crossed into the south, the Republic of Ireland, is that the white line at the edge of the road turns yellow. That's when I know we are getting close.

We drive through the town of Drogheda, it's one of the oldest towns in Ireland, some very old buildings still stand.

136

We cross the impressive bridge over the River Boyne, travel through the rest of the town and come out the other end.

We start to edge out of the town, I notice the houses getting fewer and fewer, farther and farther apart, being able to take in the scenery from the passenger seat for a change.

We reach the countryside but still no sign of a carnival in the distant view of the winding road and bumpy hills. We drive for a mile out of the town before Carl takes a turn down a narrow country road. I almost speak to question his decision but I'd be questioning myself too, neither of us know where we are going.

'I don't think anything is down here, maybe we should swing around and head back out the other way,' I suggest to him after five minutes of constant driving down this narrow country road.

'Shh,' he hushes me.

He turns the radio volume so low that it might as well be off.

We both wind down our windows, laughter and music fills the air. Around the next bend, we see the large rides of the carnival in an enormous field on our right beyond a small row of hedges.

We drive further down the road until we find an open field gate, signposted and attended by volunteer stewards of the festival in bright yellow coats.

We wait behind a small line of cars before we get inside where we are guided to a space beside other cars parked in the field.

I step out of the car into the destroyed turf and its soaked mud. I wait for Carl to come around the car and then we walk into the carnival grounds.

The event is drenched in colour, bright yellows and reds being most prominent with the others putting up a fair fight. There are acts of every description out on show. It's late evening but it's still quite light.

Despite the weather, the grounds are extremely crowded with families, young and old. Fire breathers and stilt walkers walk freely throughout the crowd, tents of every shape and description are never more than a few feet away from each offering its own unique experience or entertainment inside.

Carl and I gently push our way through the crowd towards the large tent at the very back of the complex, an enormous, hexagon-shaped tent with red and white stripes that can be seen over the top of every other tent here, a towering structure.

The smell of candy floss takes me back to when I was a kid at a carnival like this. That age when you make the unconscious choice of whether clowns are scary or funny I suppose.

Every carnival I've ever been to was always dirty, very low energy and quite often you'd walk by a once jolly clown or performer, now with smeared make-up and a cigarette in their hands. It just confirmed the reality that there is no such thing as magic or endless jolliness in life, just a front that is put on for the masses until you're left with yourself and the end of the charade.

We're almost at the tent.

I start searching the crowd, looking for that dark-haired, green-eyed girl that I lost. A lot of little faces remind me vividly of Layla that shock me, feeding me the need to run up to her and take her home. Then the head turns and I know for sure it is not her, it couldn't be her.

Carl reaches the fences, cornering off the giant red and white tent before me while I stand still in the busy crowd, looking at all the happy father and daughter duos.

'Michael!' Carl calls, snapping me out of my daydream.

I go over to the fences, we follow them to the edge of the carnival, the far end of the tent. With a quick-double check over our shoulders, we both grab hold of the fence and pull it apart.

To our luck, the fence is flimsy, it easily bends out towards us. Carl holds it stable so I can climb through to the other side after I get on the other side I do the same to help Carl.

The tent becomes eerier than before, the noise of the carnival music is now distant, here everything is quiet except the howl of the wind that ruffles the tent and it's ropes.

At the side of the tent, as opposed to the main entrance that is tied closed, I notice a small side entrance, perhaps a performer entrance. I lead the way across the grass, in front of Carl, intent on that entrance.

Then it occurs to me. We are better being predictable, I don't want it to seem like we are trying to ambush them. Everyone needs to be calm, no surprises. I divert my path, checking over my shoulder. Carl follows, gesturing his confusion.

The gap of the main entrance sways in the wind, it's large enough for us to enter into the grand set-up inside. Tiers of raised seating encircle the sand-covered floor full of circus apparatus. It is all dimly lit by sporadic, overhead lights.

139

We walk out into the middle of the floor, looking all around for someone to emerge from the shadows.

The gusts from outside invade the tent and whistle through the metal frames of the seating areas, it makes it quite cold too. There is a large archway straight ahead where the performers must come from. Beyond it is what looks to be a small corridor that leads out the back into another tent, but it's too dark to see.

'Glad to see you made it, and in good time too!' a voice calls from a distance.

Eight men armed with guns emerge from behind the seating tiers, heading them up is the voice of the man I know as Tommy.

He is in his forties with short scruffy hair and a beard to go with it. He isn't overly fat but a beer belly is visible, nesting between his blue shirt and grey trousers.

'Where is she?' I ask right away as Tommy and his men approach us.

'She's close, first I want to see what you brought me,' Tommy explains, stopping about five yards in front of us.

'You bring her out, right now, or I walk.'

'I'm afraid walking away isn't an option right now,' Tommy says, looking sideways to his henchmen to draw aim at me and Carl.

'I swear to God Tommy, she better be OK,' I tell him, stepping forward and unlocking the briefcase.

I open the case and show the contents to Tommy.

I look into Tommy's eyes, waiting for him to send one his boys as a messenger to fetch Layla but nothing follows but a still silence.

I look back at Carl, he sighs, his breathing speeding up, his shoulders raise up and drop, almost as if he knows what I'm thinking in this second.

I turn back around to look at Tommy who has remained still, his lips stiff and untroubled.

'You probably knew this deep down, somewhere in the back of your mind but you didn't want to believe it. Your wife changed everything when she called the cops, this whole thing blew up, bigger than any of us. There was no going back from that point,' Tommy explains.

'Yet you still played the charade and had me get your money,' I scorn, my face pained from the strain of what must be an ugly face of hatred.

'Had to get something from it, didn't want to waste the opportunity.'

'Where is she?'

'Your daughter is a unicorn. She's become a local celebrity thanks to the media, the hottest ticket in town. When you're on my side of the situation, that becomes a very dangerous thing. The people would call back public execution if they could, if we were caught.'

'Cut the shit and tell me what you've done with my little girl!' I shout, throwing the briefcase at him.

Tommy and his henchmen raise their arms to protect them from the briefcase then I feel a tug from behind.

Carl grabs me from behind and pushes me along, shooting at Tommy and his henchmen who then dash to take cover behind the circus apparatus.

We run for the side entrance we saw on the way in, Carl stays behind me, pushing me faster and faster towards the exit while bullets skip off the sand next to our feet.

Carl fires the final rounds from his revolver back at Tommy and his men before we exit the tent and run for the broken fence.

Taking turns, we both squeeze out through the fence.

141

Once on the other side, I see Tommy come rushing out of the giant tent. Carl drags me on, back into the busy carnival.

'They've killed her, they killed her Carl,' I panic as we enter the crowds of the carnival again.

'You don't know that, don't say that shit. We'll get her, hear me?' he tells me, stuffing the empty revolver back into his jeans.

I start to feel eyes on me, I catch men's eyes fix on me and follow as we pass. How many men does Tommy have here?

'We just need to get to the car,' Carl says.

I notice Carl take a sudden interest to something off to the side of us, then I see him get tackled to the floor. Before I have time to help him a man punches me in the side of the head.

I stumble sideways, turning to face my attacker.

Carl has managed to get up off the ground and runs to a nearby tent.

A second man joins my attacker who starts into a run after me.

I decide against a straight-up fight against two taller men and flee. I run for the carousel. It is already spinning very rapidly, blaring music and is packed full of screaming kids.

I push my way up the queue, bumping into those who refuse to move before jumping the small gate where you pay for a ticket. One of the ticket men takes chase as I run alongside the carousel, trying to match its speed to jump on.

My attacker and his friend are right behind me.

I bite down and move my legs to the point of burning pains in my muscles. I reach out and grab onto a vertical bar and jump on.

Taking the moment to catch my breath, I can see the ticket man who has given up running and now stands with his hands on his hips, tilting his head in all sorts of angles looking at the carousel, looking for me.

My two pursuers come into view, still chasing the carousel. I get away from the edge and start to weave in and out of the toy horses of the ride.

Between the flashing lights, horses and gleeful kids, I spot one of the men now on board. I stay low and follow him on his slow and careful search.

I wait until we reach a pair of empty horses with no kids before I strike.

I stand up behind him, grabbing the back of his head and drive it into the hard body of the nearest horse. I repeat the action twice more as hard as I can before I trail him, staggering to the edge and throw him off the ride.

A frantic cry of screams follows the fall of the bloodied man from the ride.

The music on the ride stops and it starts to slow down, they must've shut it off. I catch the sight of the other man further down the platform. I duck down and begin to get swarmed by the sea of kids getting off the ride amidst groans and complaints.

The man continues further around the platform on the other side of the ride. I stick with the crowd, staying low and get off the platform.

Once on the grass, I glance back to see the man walking towards the fence where the parents wait, I break off and run between the back of the tents ahead.

143

I dodged that bullet. Shit, Carl, I need to find him. I hope he is OK.

I'm more careful of crowds now, weighing up each one before joining it from the shelter of tent entrances. I can't see him anywhere. I see a group of rough men, covered in tattoos and sporting bomber jackets come into view.

I retreat to the cover of another tent entrance.

I stand and wait until they pass.

Once they are out of view I put my lead foot out to take a step but I am pulled backwards into the tent. I land on the dirty carpet floor and look up to see my brother's face.

'We need to get the hell out of here, they're everywhere,' Carl says, now baring a few cuts and bruises.

He goes over to a table that has been draped in numerous colourful materials. I get back to my feet and watch him search through the pile. He drags out an outfit from the pile and carries it back to me.

'Here, put this on,' he tells me, holding up a clown outfit.

'You're joking,' I tell him, taking the outfit in my hands.

'Not a great time to be joking,' he says.

We exit the tent a few minutes later, me dressed in a clown outfit that is way too big for me while Carl has picked out an animal outfit.

We mix in with the crowd and filter towards the car park.

The car park has expanded, making it hard to pinpoint where we have parked.

We split up, taking an aisle each to find the car.

It doesn't take long before Carl starts flagging me over. We take off our suits and leave them in the mud. I get into the driver's seat before Carl gets the chance to bid for it.

We drive out of the field and I pull up into a lay-by on the road outside the entrance gate. The adrenaline subsides and I feel a pain slowly building in my leg.

'What are you doing?' Carl asks as I switch off the engine.

'I'm gonna wait for this bastard and then I'm going to follow him back to Layla.'

The rain pelts the windscreen hard before it becomes hail. The sky has started to darken and the lights from the carnival become more prominent. We wait there, listening to the static of the radio as a radio presenter tries to break through it.

Carl shifts in his seat, he takes the revolver out of his jeans and puts it into the glove box.

I hear a rumbling noise, then I feel it. It's my phone. I brace myself, readying my words for Tommy and take the phone out of my pocket, but it's not Tommy calling.

I answer the call from Naomi.

'Hello?'

'I assume you and your brother are both there?' a man's voice questions. I know that voice.

I place the phone next to the gear stick and put it on loudspeaker.

'We're both here,' I confirm.

'Naomi is a beautiful woman, a love interest of one of you I assume?' Chester mocks.

'What do you want?' Carl asks.

'Simple, the rest of the coke.'

'Don't you even dare fucking touch her,' Carl scolds.

'Come get her. You know where we are,' Chester mocks again.

'She has nothing to do with this, leave her out of it. We've got your bags in the boot. We're in the car now,' Carl says.

'You do, eh? That's great news. Carl, I presume? Unfortunately, Carl, she is part of this now. You can thank your brother Michael for that. You made the mistake of leaving your friend Andy alive in that alley. He gave your new address up. You should have put a bullet in his head to save me using my own. A man will do or say anything to save his family from harm. Anyway, gotta run. Kettle is boiled. You could really do with a new sofa by the way, this one is ripped to shit. See you soon,' Chester says before hanging up.

Carl adjusts in his seat and then starts bashing the dashboard with the palm of his hand.

'OK, let's go!' he says.

I ignore him, keeping my eyes focused on the road, before diverting to the field gate of the carnival in my rearview mirror.

'What's wrong? Let's go! Start it up,' Carl says.

I remain still, keeping my eyes on that gate

'Michael—'

'What Carl! What?' I explode.

'Naomi needs us, we need to get there now.'

'What about Tommy? What about Layla?'

Carl rolls his eyes and leans his elbow on the door putting his head in his hand.

We sit in silence for a minute before Carl straightens up to reason with me again.

'We'll come back for him and we'll get her. I promise you that.'

'We're out of time, if I lose him now, we lose her too.'

'What if she's already gone?'

146

I look Carl in the eyes, he has started to turn red, his voice becoming increasingly more emotional.

I punch him in the face for suggesting such a notion.

He slowly turns his face back around to me, his lower lip starting to bleed.

He checks his lip with his hand which gets bloodied.

He sighs.

'I'm sorry, I shouldn't have said that.' Carl explains.

I don't bare to consider it. It's an unthinkable outcome. I open the car door to get out, to get away from Carl but I can't risk exposing myself.

I slam it shut again, rocking the car.

Whimpers begin coming from Carl before he lets it out and starts to weep.

His face turns red, and tears flow down his cheeks before he hides it in his hands.

'Please Michael, you're my brother, I'm begging you to help me. You wouldn't have gotten this far on your own.'

He's right but I can't let go of the chance to tail Tommy back to where he is hiding out. Layla is depending on me.

'I can't,' I tell him softly.

'Yes you can, you're in the position you can help me, Naomi and Layla. But you can't get Layla back without my help, you know that. And if you want my help, you need to stop and help me now.'

I stay silent. Through his tears and sniffling, Carl utters three more words.

'I love her.'

I've never seen my brother cry before, not as an adult. It's unsettling. He's gone through all this shit with me, despite me being the cause of it.

He's never wavered, never hesitated or tried to walk away. I need him, I need his help to pull this off. Chester is gonna keep coming for us until he gets a trunk full of coke or puts a bullet in our heads. Naomi is another being held as collateral for my actions.

I glance at the gate once more in the rearview.

It's become a still image in my mind as I continue to drive. It may turn out to be a reminder of a decision. A decision I don't know will be right or wrong.

I turn on the engine and Carl raises his head up out of his hands, I see an instant change in him as he knows what the noise of the engine signifies.

'Let's go get these bastards,' I tell him.

He sits back in his seat and nods, biting his lip.

We pull out of the lay-by and drive up the narrow country road.

***

The drive back seems twice as quick as coming down. I constantly check the rearview mirror, not for cars. I dwell on the thought of leaving Layla back there with every mile but I have to hold on the faith that she is safe and that Tommy wants more than the money. I'm holding on to the hope he wants me dead, the thick thorn in his side.

He knows that I still know things, things I didn't share with the cops the first time, the only reason he's not on the inside.

We don't make any stops on the ride to Carl's apartment, not for food, not for petrol as the arrow reaches the red marker, or even for the idea of arming ourselves.

We will need to think on our feet walking into this trap set for us.

'I think I've got something for when we get up here,' I tell him.

'What are you thinking?' Carl asks, all ears for any ideas.

We reach Tullycarnet and pull into the street in front of the apartment. We park up, no double-checking, no over-evaluation of our surroundings, we just get out of the car and walk inside, no-nonsense.

We climb the stairs side by side until we reach his door.

Carl knocks and we wait for an answer.

A bulky man answers and stands aside for us to come in, we enter.

The bulking man closes the door behind us, guarding it. We walk up the small hallway, two men stand by the kitchen door ahead, armed with automatic rifles in their hands.

We go in through the open door of the living room to find Chester stood by the television, leaning on his good leg and another one of his men sat on the sofa, looking up at us with a serious look on his face. Me and Carl exchange stares with them until Chester speaks.

'Welcome home boys.'

'Where is she?' Carl asks.

'In the bedroom, where is the coke? Not kind enough to bring it up?' Chester asks.

'It's safe in the car. Show us, Naomi, first then you get the keys.'

'Feel free,' Chester says, pointing to the living room door.

Carl leaves and goes to the bedroom, leaving me standing alone facing Chester.

'She OK?' I shout to Carl.

'Yeah,' he replies.

I pull the keys from my pocket and hold them outstretched to Chester.

'Joseph, go check out the car.'

The man sitting on the sofa gets up and snatches the keys out of my hand before leaving the apartment.

I hear Carl's bedroom door open again.

'Mind if I make a cup of tea?' Carl shouts in sarcastic glee.

'Make yourself at home!' Chester shouts back in equal glee.

'Would you like one yourself?' asks Carl, his footsteps moving towards the kitchen.

'No thanks, not staying long,' Chester answers, a sinister undertone detected in his answer.

Chester takes a seat on the sofa as the bulky man comes into the living room to keep an eye on me. I smile at him and then focus my eyes back on Chester.

A high pitched screeching rings throughout the building, the sprinklers overhead start shooting out jets of water, catching everyone in the room by surprise apart from me.

I tackle the big bulky man out into the hall and onto the ground. I drive three quick elbows into his face, knocking him out.

The two men at the kitchen door wipe the water from their eyes and run at me, weapons raised. The first one stops, standing over me and takes aim at my head.

Behind him, I see Carl tackling his friend into the wall, driving something into his chest. The man standing over me drops his gun. His face turns expressionless and he drops on his face on the floor next to me.

A knife sticks out of his back of his neck. I turn my eyes down the hallway, seeing Carl standing still after throwing

150

the knife. He looks to his side, checking the other man who is slumped against the wall on the ground.

I get to my feet and we both enter the living room.

'She OK?' I ask Carl.

'Yeah,' he says.

We enter the living room to find Chester hiding behind the armchair in the corner of the room.

'Let me walk and I'll forget about all of this,' he pleads.

Me and Carl close in on him.

'You don't want my friends coming after you. They'll really go to work on you. Not just you, your families, your kids. If you have any pets, they'll kill them too.'

Carl launches at him, grabbing him and dragging him out from behind the chair. He drags him into the middle of the floor with Chester crawling on all fours, being dragged by the collar.

Carl lets go of him and Chester gets to his feet, running for the door but I block his path.

'Get out of my way!' he screams in my face.

I shove him, sending him stumbling backwards. Finding his feet, he turns and takes a wild swing at Carl. Carl dodges it and counter punches him, sending him into the television which is knocked off the stand and crashes to the floor.

'Get Naomi and take her to the car. I'll be down in a minute,' he says without taking his eyes off Chester who gets slowly back to his feet with a busted lip.

I leave the room, going to Carl's bedroom where Naomi is hid behind the bed.

'Naomi, c'mon, we've gotta go.'

'What about Carl?' she asks, getting up.

'He's gonna meet us down there, he's OK.'

I grab the bag of guns under the bed and lead her out of the apartment without looking back. We start descending the stairs of the apartment block. We go down them as quick as we can, misplacing steps in our rush and almost tripping.

Our footsteps echo down through the building until I start to notice they are out of sync. I hold my arm out in front of Naomi.

'Wait,' I whisper to her.

The footsteps continue as we stand still.

It's Chester's guy on the way back up from the car.

We need to get the keys back.

I signal for Naomi to stay quiet and stay where she is.

I hand over the bag of guns to her before I venture onwards on my own down the stairs. I start running down the stairs to meet him. I spot the blue of his jumper as I turn on the stair landing.

I jump down the flight of stairs at him, I clash with him in mid-air, taking him by surprise. We roll together down the remaining stairs until the next landing where the momentum of the fall stops.

I get to my feet first and start punching and kicking him before he starts to fight back. I reach out, taking a few of his punches on the way in, and grab him by the throat, pushing him against the wall.

He breaks my grip on his neck and starts to push my face away. I stomp on his feet to try to unbalance him but it doesn't work. Instead, he catches me off balance and takes me to the ground. He gets into a dominant position and starts to strike from on top of me.

I reach out in an attempt to catch his strikes but one gets through. It rocks me, I get dazed, then I'm not sure what's going on.

152

I see Naomi appearing above us, attacking the guy, trying to get him off me.

He stands up, knowing he's dealt with me and he grabs Naomi, pushing her out of sight. I roll over, putting my hands on the ground, trying to get up. I feel light-headed, all of my strength diminished. I try using my arms to push myself up onto my knee which I get under me but I can't. I almost crash to the ground again but I grab hold of the handrail of the stairs. I use both of my hands to pull myself up to my feet it.

I hear Naomi screaming, my focus starts to come back, my head starts to clear. I see the guy pushing Naomi up against the handrail a couple of yards up the stairs. I go up and grab the guy from behind, dragging him away from Naomi.

He struggles hard. I slam him, stomach first into the handrail. I keep him pressed against it, judging what my next move should be.

Naomi comes down the stairs past us with the gun bag in hand. The guy surprises me, a burst of energy as he launches for Naomi as she passes.

I retain control of him, stopping him from narrowly grabbing Naomi and swing him back around towards the railing, using all of my strength. I swing his stomach into the railing so hard that he folds over it and falls three stories, I fall into the rail and watch him drop, screaming and flailing his arms and legs until they cut out like a record.

The sickening thud of his body hitting the ground and rolling from the impact on the ground floor.

I take a breath and continue down the stairs, finding Naomi knelt down, her eyes blackened from the mixture of tears and mascara.

Her mouth opens and closes, wanting to cry out but her voice breaks. I pick up the bag of guns and put a comforting arm around her, helping her up again and slowly escort her down the stairs.

When we reach the final flight of stairs I shield her eyes with one hand, to protect her from the sight of the man's body on the ground. We leave the stairs and I guide Naomi to the door before removing my hand from her eyes.

'Go out to the car and wait for me there, I have to get the key OK?' I say to her softly.

She nods, wiping the tears from her eyes.

She goes out of the building and walks to the car. I go back to the body on the floor and start searching through his pockets for the car key. I get the key from his pocket and leave the building.

Naomi is standing beside the car when I cross the road to her.

I open the car, letting her get into the back seat but I don't get in. I stop and look up at the window of Carl's apartment for any sight of him.

There is nothing in the window apart from the edge of the curtains, no movement inside. I wait for something to happen, the front door to open, someone appearing at the window, just anything, but nothing happens in those first two minutes that seem like ten. I open Naomi's door and hand her the car key.

'Take these, I need to go get him. If anyone comes, get outta here.'

'Michael—' she says before I shut the door on her.

I put the bag of guns in the boot and go back towards the building. That's when the front door opens and Carl comes marching out.

I stop in my tracks and wait for him.

'C'mon! It's done. Let's go,' he says when he gets close.

I get into the car before Carl, taking the key back off Naomi.

Carl gets in and we get out of there.

'Drop Naomi off at her mum's house,' Carl instructs me.

'Where's that?' I ask, driving blind.

'Lisburn, I'll give you directions once we get there.'

'Why am I going there? I want to stay with you,' Naomi protests to Carl.

'There's no way. I'm not gonna risk you getting hurt,' he tells her, turning in his seat to face back at her.

'I'm not letting you do this on your own. I may not be able to do much but I don't want to let you get hurt.'

'This isn't about me, or you, or us,' Carl tells her, I feel the focus shift to me and the elephant in the room.

***

Carl directs me to Naomi's mum's house.

Carl walks her to the front door and they exchange the second goodbye of the same day and a parting kiss.

When Carl gets back in I start driving back to Belfast.

'What's the plan? Where are we going? You look like you know something I don't,' Carl asks.

'I have an idea. We need to go to my house and get a phone number I have hidden away in an old notepad,' I tell him.

We get to the house and check around the street before getting out.

To our luck, everything is quiet, not even a dog walker out and about.

We go up to the door and I retrieve a spare key that was always hidden under a plant pot. I had got the idea of the spare key after a toxic night out. I lost my keys in the bar and attempted to break into my own house around five in the morning. The house was locked up tight and all of the windows were closed, except for one.

The bathroom window at the side of the house was slightly ajar so I tried my luck with it, dragging over an old bag of concrete to stand on to reach it. Skip ahead an hour, there I am with my ass sticking out of the window and my torso hanging on the inside with two cops checking me out from the garden, laughing hysterically at me. Lisa raised the alarm after she heard my cries of pain from being stuck following my loud swearing, she thought we were getting burgled.

Thankfully the locks haven't been changed. They must've gotten the keys from Lisa.

Once me and Carl get in, we go into the living room and start hunting through the stack of shelves by the house phone for the blue notepad with Colin's number. He helped me get the guns at the start of this and told me he couldn't play any other part but it's not a choice any more.

I find the notepad and pull it out from between two large hardback books. I lay it on the sofa and start flicking through the pages, Carl watches over my shoulder.

I find the page and track down it until I reach Colin's number scribbled in red ink opposed to the rest that are in black.

I lift the house phone but Carl slams my hand and the phone back down.

'You stupid?' he asks rhetorically.

'I forgot myself there,' I admit, forgetting the obvious fact that a call from this house may flag up on the police radar.

I key the number into my mobile and ring it.

'Hello?' Colin answers.

'Colin, it's Michael.'

'Michael, I told you, I can't have any part in this.'

'Is Layla still alive?'

'What? What do you mean?'

'I mean do you know if she is still alive? I met Tommy for the exchange and she wasn't there. He got on like they got rid of her.'

'Michael, I swear on my life that I don't know anything. I'm only back from Paris with the Missus.'

'Listen, I need your help again.'

'Michael...'

'I'm out of time and I'm out of options. I know that you are in the know. I need the names of the guys who played a part in taking Layla.'

'I think you forget who you are talking to. I owed you one but I sorted you out with the guns, guns to be used against my own crew. But now, we are even. Don't call me, don't associate my name with your own, we're done.'

Colin hangs up.

It was the kind of response I expected, but I had to give him the option first, the choice to help but now it's a choice that I'll have to force upon him.

'What now then?' Carl asks.

'We get ready,' I tell him.

I start to take notice of how worn our clothes have become, covered in spatters of blood here and there from our ordeals. I take off my t-shirt and throw it on the floor.

'Let's go up and get some new clothes, these ones are done,' I tell him.

We go up to my wardrobe and pick out an outfit each. Carl takes a pair of black trousers, a t-shirt and a jumper to go over it, half black, half green.

I take out a pair of jeans and throw a leather jacket over a dark blue hoody.

Carl goes to leave but I call him back.

'Wait a minute,' I tell him.

'What is it?' he asks, coming back.

I slide the clothes across on their hangers until I reach my collection of suits hung up.

'Pick one of these out for yourself.'

'What for?' he asks.

'Just pick one out, you'll need it.'

He reluctantly picks a black suit.

I pick one of the other suits, which also happens to be black.

'Where to now?' Carl asks.

'An old friend's for a bit of persuasion.'

'That guy that was one the phone? Him?' he asks.

'Yeah, we're heading to Dublin.'

A sudden noise from downstairs freezes me and Carl to the spot.

We look at each other whilst listening out for any other sound to come from downstairs.

We slowly creep out of the bedroom, sticking close together and peer down the stairs from over the wooden bannister. We can't see anything, nothing apart from the glow of the street lights coming through the glass of the front door, hitting the bottom steps.

I'm about to put the noise down to nothing until I hear a door creaking open. I know for a fact it's the living room door, it's the only door that creaks in the house. Someone is down there. I take the lead on the way down the stairs, lowering my feet gently onto each step as to not make any noise that might give us away to the intruder. I keep my eye on the living room door as it comes into view on the descent. It is open, showing the light of the living room beyond.

We get down into the hallway and a cold draft starts to hit my legs. That's when me and Carl notice that the front door is slightly ajar. Then a sort of scuffling starts coming from the living room. We edge up to the door. We stop and listen for a moment when someone comes out in front of us, into the hallway. I'm closest to the door so I make the first move, grabbing him by the neck and forcing him backwards into the wall. He is a tall man, slightly taller than me with a skinny frame and dark, thick-framed glasses.

'Ahh! Y-you know this house is off-limits?' he stutters, trying to sound threatening with a trembling voice.

'Graham? What are you doing in here?' I ask.

The voice gave him away, I should have known from his tall, skinny frame and nerdy glasses, he's my next-door neighbour. He has always been the nosey type. The self-righteous do-gooder of the neighbourhood.

'I thought there were kids in here trying to steal things, so I came in to scare them off.'

A short laugh bursts out from Carl.

'What?' Graham asks defensively.

'Well, to be honest. The only people you would scare, would be parents in a playground.'

'Fuck, Carl. That's a bit dark,' I say.

Carl shrugs his shoulders with a smile. I turn my focus back to Graham.

'I need you to keep quiet about us being in here, OK?' I tell Graham.

'But, aren't the cops after you for the disappearance of your daughter?'

'Yeah, which is why I need you to keep quiet. It's complicated.'

'Well, I think I will need to call the police and let them decide,' he says.

He reaches for his pocket, I assume for his phone. I grab his wrist and stop his hand from entering his pocket.

'I'd really appreciate if you didn't,' I say more assertively than before.

'Let my hand go, David,' he says back in his own firm tone.

He wriggles his hand back and forth, trying to break my grip.

'Let go of my hand, David!' he says again, raising his voice.

Carl comes in from the side with a fast and heavy punch to Graham's face. He drops instantly, hitting the floor and going limp.

'What the hell was that?' I ask Carl, taken aback.

'Call it instinct. He was gonna call the cops no matter what we said. He would've followed us out and got the plates of Naomi's car.'

He has a good point. We can't sabotage our only car. He wouldn't have noticed it on the way in from where we have parked it.

160

'What do we do with him now?' Carl asks.

'We do nothing, we leave him here then we get out, now before he wakes up.'

'What if he wakes up while we are taking stuff out to the car?'

'How long will he be out for?'

'I don't know.'

'What do you mean you don't know?'

'I've never knocked anyone out before so I don't know.'

'You've never knocked anyone out before?'

'No, have you?'

'No, but, should he not be out a long time?'

'All depends.'

'Fuck!' I exclaim as I start to pace the hall.

'What do you want to do with him then?' I ask Carl.

'Blindfold the lanky twat and throw him in the boot. Drive him out to the country and dump him off. He won't know where he is or where we have gone. Take his phone,' Carl says as he makes a move to pick Graham up off the floor.

Once everything, including Graham, is in the car, we use one of my old ties as a make-shift blindfold on him while he is still out cold.

'Wait a minute,' Carl says, reaching into the boot at Graham's feet.

'What are you doing?' I ask.

Carl undoes the laces on Graham's shoes and takes them off, throwing them into the back seat.

'It'll take him a bit longer getting to a phone barefoot,' he says before slamming the boot closed.

'You've got a twisted mind you know that?' I tell him before we get into the car.

161

***

We drive out into the hills and then the country until it is pitch black. There is nothing but fields around us and even these roads are beaten up country roads, no wider than the car. It's close to midnight so there are no cars on the roads.

We find a place to stop next to a large field with no houses around, and we get out. We open the boot to see Graham is still lying there motionless.

'You sure you didn't kill him?' I ask Carl, seriously.

Carl reaches down and grabs hold of Graham's legs and they spring to life. Carl gets kicked in the face and he falls back onto the ground next to me holding his nose.

Graham sits up and scrambles to get out of the car with the blindfold still on. I grab him as he falls out of the car, the momentum takes us both to the ground. He continues to wiggle and squirm on the ground and I lose my grip on him.

He gets up and runs blindly towards a gate of the field next to us.

He sprints into it at full speed, smashing into it stomach first and then flipping over it into the field.

Me and Carl both get to our feet and go over to the gate to look down on Graham who is laid in the mud groaning from pain and holding his stomach.

The tie is still around his eyes, must've been tighter than I thought.

'Let's go,' Carl says, patting me on the shoulder and jogging back to the car. We leave Graham there and drive out onto the narrow country roads.

***

Taking the A1 carriageway directly to Dublin. We stop at a service station on the way. It's the early hours of the morning.

We decide to stop and get a few hours of sleep in the car and wait for the morning until we go to see Colin.

DAY SIX

We wake up to being surrounded by a convoy of large trucks who have pulled into the service station, it's quite busy. We both get a coffee from inside the shop before setting off for Dublin.

There are so many lanes on the outer motorway of Dublin, it's very easy to get caught in the wrong one, even losing direction. I've travelled these roads so many times I'm luckily immune to such mistakes.

We travel to a place called Summerhill, an area in north, inner-city, Dublin. It's not too dissimilar to Belfast's streets, roads and architecture, sometimes tricking me into thinking it is part of Belfast until I see the road signs. On the way, I have a lot of time to think. My thoughts drift on how I first came to meet with and get involved with Colin - the man who brought me into the underworld.

I was eighteen and very heavily involved in the drug scene.

I had left school with barely any qualifications and struggled to hold any job longer than three months. The company I kept didn't help my situation. They were all the same as me, wasters, spending most of their time spaced out in Danny's living room.

Then came the one night that woke me up.

***

It was the usual Saturday night.

Danny worked in a call centre. As soon as he finished his shift, we would pick him up and drive back to his house. Peter was the only one of us that had a car, he was our chauffeur.

We all got back to Danny's around ten that night, he finished his shift at half nine. There was four of us; me, Danny, Peter and Ricky. But this Saturday night turned out to be a little different, a bit special.

'So what were you talking about on the phone earlier?' I asked Danny.

'Wait till ya see,' he told me, opening up his backpack as we all get into the living room.

He pulled out three large see-through bags, filled with some sort of white pills.

He took each bag out one by one and threw them onto the glass coffee table in front of the sofas.

'Wow, what are these little demons?' Ricky asked as he lifted up a bag in glee.

'These, my friends, are the purest ecstasy pills doing the rounds right now,' Danny said proudly.

'Where the hell did you get these? How much where they? Must've been a fortune,' Peter said, also grabbing a bag to examine.

'Nope got em for free.'

'How?' I ask.

'Fella in my work is selling them for someone, but he's a bitch. Caught him out during my smoke break and basically told him, if he didn't give me everything he had, I'd knock him out,' Danny laughed.

'Have you tried them yet?' Peter asked.

Danny shook his head and then picked up one of the bags, reached inside and took two pills out.

166

'Let's get the ball rolling!' he shouted before swallowing them both.

We all decided to follow suit, taking two pills each. It took about fifteen minutes to have any effect.

We put on the television and put on the boxing fight.

It got to round two and the pills hit me. I felt a cold shiver run up my body and my blood turned to ice one second, the next a warm feeling.

Soon, we are were all feeling the effects, that's when we start into the gin and whiskey stockpiled in the kitchen cupboards. Soon, the conversation started to shift to the idea of heading out to a club. We listed out all of the places we could hit and debated the pros and cons of each, all undecided on where to go before it got too late to get in.

We finally settled on one and Peter was left to ring the taxi. He went off to the toilet to ring one, away from the noise of us, the television and the loud music of Danny's old CD player. He had recently decided it would be a great idea to start playing one of his old clubland CDs to everyone's protest.

Laying back on the sofa, I started hearing a loud thud through all of the noise. But I ignored it, could be anything. I started listening in to Danny and Rick's conversation on dinosaurs and evolution when I heard it again.

This time, it was loud enough that Rick and Danny could hear it too.

They stop for a moment in silence.

'Peter must be pushing out dam busters up there!' Ricky jokes.

He and Danny laughed but it quickly disappeared when the thuds rang out again and for longer this time.

Danny gets up and cautiously moves over to the CD player, turning the music down so low that it may as well have been off. We all sat still, listening for it again.

The thuds returned, loud and thunderous, obviously coming from the front door.

Danny got a dose of bravery and stands up.

'Who the fuck is that banging on my front door?' he shouted, storming out into the hallway.

Me and Ricky listened carefully as Danny unlocked the door, we hear the creak of it opening.

'What do you want?' Danny's voice all of a sudden timid.

There was a scuffle in the hallway, what sounded like a fight. I launched up out of the sofa, rushing to Danny's aid.

When I looked into the hallway, I saw three masked men beating Danny on the floor with iron bars. They stopped and looked at me. One of them reaches for something in their coat and mutters 'C'mere!'

I shut the living room door and ran to the back door.

'Get out. C'mon!' I shouted to Ricky but he sat still. I stopped at the kitchen door to usher him on but the living room door burst open and two masked men entered. I turned and ran, throwing open the back door and sprinting for the wooden fence.

I hear the back door swing open and hit the wall again once I reach the grass, they were behind me. I threw myself up onto the fence and fell over into the garden on the other side. I got to my feet as quick as I could with mud all over my clothes, and ran for the side of the house.

I got out onto the street and kept running, trying to put distance between me, the house and the masked men. I turned the corner onto another street and stopped to catch my breath. Looking back down the street I came from, I couldn't see anybody. I started walking, I had to keep moving, I couldn't stay around there.

The streets were quiet and empty, not even a car on the roads. There were distant shouts and yells from the nearby houses. It was Saturday night, after all, there must have been a few house parties going on.

My heart stopped and I restarted at a sprinting pace as I heard the roars of an engine far behind me. I looked over my shoulder for a split second to catch a glimpse of the distant headlights of a slow-moving car. I looked ahead and already started to plan my escape route should I need it. It was a very straight road, I'd have been completely fucked in a race.

There were no more side streets, just gardens but nowhere to go as all of the houses were semi-detached with no side entrance to the back garden, just brick walls. I really started to panic as I heard the car getting closer.

I start to misstep and almost tripped as my walking speed up. There was no way someone would drive at that speed normally.

Whoever it was, I had a feeling they had bad intentions. I started to hit the pavement hard, dashing.

The car behind roared its engine again and speed up after me. My eyes skipped between this side of the street and the other, begging for a way out. Then I found it. An alleyway up ahead on my side. The car caught up, almost right alongside me before I turned down into the alley.

The brakes of the car screeched behind me and the car doors swung open. The muscles in my legs started to burn, I wouldn't be able to keep up this pace the entire length of the alleyway.

I stopped and turned, facing the two masked men running down after me. I placed my feet, getting into a fighting stance to take them on when they got to me. To my luck, only one of them still had an iron bar, he's the one who reached me first. He took one wild swing which I ducked under. I grabbed his arm, twisting the bar out of it and head-butted him. I got one swing at his head before his friend was on me.

We stood up off each other, I had the upper hand having the bar. He made a grab for it.

We wrestled for control of it, he even kicked me in the gut but I wouldn't let go. If I did he'd beat me senseless. I stole it back, swinging at him, mostly hitting his arm which he had raised up to protect himself. I beat him the whole way to the ground. Swing, after swing until the gunshot.

I'd never heard one in real life but it was unmistakable that the blast came from a gun. I rose up, getting away from both the masked men and looked beyond them to see a third walking towards me with his gun aimed.

The other two got slowly up off the floor and came for me. They punched and kicked me into the wall of the alley. The third broke in between both of them and grabbed me by the collar.

I felt an ice-cold metal object pushed into my cheek, that's when I clicked on that it was the gun.

'Here, wait a minute, hang on,' a fourth masked man said arriving on the scene.

He came up close, taking a good look at me.

'Put him into the car,' he said.

I tried my best to break free but they struggled with me the whole way back down the alley and pushed me into the back seat of a black car. I didn't know what to think.

170

Maybe they were taking me somewhere quieter to finish me off. Who were they? Two of them get into the back seat beside me. It was not until he talked, that I realised that the one sitting next to me was the fourth man who spoke.

'You run about with some dickheads Michael,' he told me.

'What's this all about?' I asked.

He took off his mask, I recognised him. Colin. We had gone to the same high school together. He was a few years above me.

'Colin?'

'Your mate stole a backpack full of product from one of our guys,' he told me.

'Your guys?' I asked.

'Yeah, don't worry. I know you didn't have anything to do with it, but do yourself a favour, stay away from those junkies.'

'What happens now?' I asked, pondering on where we were going.

'You work?' he asked me.

'Kind of, in a bakery doing shifts at the minute.'

'Good money?'

'Shit,' I told him.

'If you ever want to make some real money, give me a call. We might be able to work something out. We know you can handle yourself anyway,' he said, laughing slightly with the rest of them in the car.

He leaned forward, tapping the driver on the shoulder.

'Here will do,' he said to the driver.

I feel the car slowing down as Colin sat back down in his seat.

I took his number down in my phone as the car came to a stop in a random street I didn't recognise. I got out and stepped onto the footpath. Colin shifted over, taking my seat.

'You didn't see anything tonight,' he told me in a serious tone.

'Got it,' I said, nodding back to him.

He shut the car door and it raced off down the street.

***

I stuck to Colin's advice and stayed away from Danny and the rest of the guys. Spending all of my time and focus on working extra shifts at the bakery, so much extra time that I didn't have time for much else.

Each day started to bleed into the next and the wage at the end of the week didn't even seem to justify the amount of work I put in. I started to grow frustrated at my situation. I wouldn't really jump ship into any other job that would be any more satisfying or better paid as I didn't have the qualifications or experience.

The idea of giving Colin a call started to play on my mind. I knew it would be stupid to get involved with them kind of guys but I kept thinking of the money.

I also kept thinking of the thrill I had when they chased me that night and I managed to take them on single-handedly. I had finished my last late shift of the week at the bakery, packing the vans full of boxes for the deliveries the next day.

Another hour of chasing up and filling in paperwork follows before I finally pulled down the shutters and headed home for the night.

The entire walk home, I recounted the events of that night at Danny's, and of Colin's offer. It got too good in my mind to pass up. For the rest of the way home, in my head, I started to run through how the conversation would go.

I got into my mum and dad's house and make myself a cup of coffee. The house was empty, everyone must be away to bed but someone had forgotten to turn off the television and all of the lights were still on. I sipped on the coffee and got Colin's number up on my phone. I stared at the call button, anxious about pressing it.

Is it too late at night to call him?

Will he remember the offer? Was it genuine?

I started to question everything, maybe trying to find an excuse to get rid of the anxiety by not calling. I decided I couldn't chicken out now. I went out the back to make sure no one would listen in or come down the stairs in the middle of the conversation.

I finished my coffee first amidst the pacing of the garden and press dial. It started ringing. It rang to the point where I thought I should have hung up but I stayed on the line.

My persistence paid off when he answered.

'Hello, who is this?'

'Colin, it's Michael.'

'Michael?'

'O'Connell. I got your number a couple of weeks back.'

'Yes! Michael! Sorry, I forgot about that. You thought about the offer then?'

'Yeah, I want in.'

'Good, you free tomorrow night? Might need you.'

173

'Yeah.'

'Perfect. I'll give you a call closer to the time. This your number?'

'Yeah, it's my mobile.'

'Keep it close tomorrow after seven and I'll call by and pick you up.'

'Sounds good.'

'Talk to you soon, bud.'

'OK, cya.'

'Bye,' he said before hanging up.

I finished my shift early at the bakery the next day, knocking off at six and went home to wait for the call.

Around ten to seven, I stood and waited outside of my house. I didn't want mum or dad seeing who I was going out with and I didn't want Colin calling to the door either.

It was bang on seven, and still no sign of him or a call. I looked up and down the street, staring at every car that came up the road but they never stopped. It was four minutes past, has something gone wrong? Something came up or was it off?

I was about to head back inside and watch the road from the bedroom window when my phone finally rang.

Colin told me he was just around the corner and to come outside. I told him I was already outside and I stepped out of the garden and onto the footpath. I hung up and then the headlights of Colin's car turned the corner into my street, parking up right in front of me. I got in and he started to drive again.

'Alright, all good?' he asked.

'Yeah, yeah.'

'Good. Doing a little pick-up tonight, nothing big, just need an extra set of eyes and maybe another pair of hands, should go down without a problem though.'

'OK, no problem,' I told him.

'OK, it's gonna take about fifteen-minutes to get there and then we need to drive for another hour to the drop-off point, that OK with you? You don't have to be anywhere tonight do you?' he asked, politely to my surprise.

'No, I'm freed up.'

Colin drove us to the other side of Belfast.

I had rarely visited this part of the city, everything we pass was like a new sight, a new discovery to me. A part of the city mostly unknown to me.

We stopped outside a house.

It looked a mess. The front garden was overgrown, the front gate was rusted and hanging off its hinges and the wooden front door had holes and gashes in it.

'Take the wheel, keep the engine running, I won't be long,' Colin said to me.

We both got out of the car and passed each other as we both went around the front of the car in opposite directions.

I got into the driver's seat and watched him go up and knock on the door. A bearded man in sweat bottoms answered the door, rubbing his scruffy hair and talking to Colin. He moved aside, letting Colin inside and slammed the door shut. I turned the radio up a little for something to keep my mind occupied.

I waited for around five minutes until Colin emerged from the house again. He put something into the back seat before getting into the passenger seat.

'OK, go,' he told me.

I start to drive.

175

'Where are we going?' I asked.

'Just drive,' Colin told me, checking the mirrors.

He didn't speak again until we reached the centre of Belfast.

'You gonna tell me where we are going yet?' I asked finally.

'Take me back home, I'll finish this tomorrow,' Colin said, grabbing a bag from the back seat and clutching it in his arms.

I kept my eyes on the car behind us as we weaved through the streets of the city centre. I first noticed it when we had left the house that Colin went in to, it's been following our every move but now it was closing in, closer and closer behind us.

'I think we have a tail,' I told Colin.

He checked the mirrors, looking at the car behind us. 'What are you talking about?'

'I'm serious, I'm not fucking around, it's been following us since we left that house.'

'You're being paranoid Michael, it's OK, it's your first job, I get it.'

'No, listen to me, I'm not being paranoid, it's definitely following us. You should get out on the next turn. I'll lure them away.'

'Are you losing the plot? Just shut up and drive.'

'What's in the bag?' I asked, looking over at it on his lap.

'Don't you worry about the bag, worry about the road.'

'What's in the bag?' I demanded again.

'If you don't calm down, I swear Michael, you'll regret it.'

A loud screech startled us both and flashes of blue light ignite the inside of the car.

In my mirror, I saw the siren, hidden in the grill of the car following us. It was an unmarked cop car.

I stepped on the accelerator and begun racing through the busy streets with Colin grabbing hold of the dashboard.

'Shake him!' Colin shouted to me.

I tried my best to outmanoeuvre the car, but I only gained a little ground with it hot on our heels.

I raced back towards our part of the city, towards the waterfront of Belfast. I took a slight scenic route, handbrake turning into a narrow road leading to the cathedral quarter. I slammed on the breaks and reached across for Colin's door handle.

'What are you doing?' he asked as I did it.

I pushed his door open and quickly shoved him out of the car and onto the pavement. I raced off without giving him an answer. The blue flashing lights soon found me again. I lead them towards the bridge over the River Lagan. I spotted out of the corner of my eye that Colin's bag had been left behind. I reached my hand over to open it whilst keeping a firm grip of the wheel with the other.

I managed to unzip it and grabbed a white packaged block.

I've seen enough films to know it's cocaine.

Shit.

We got closer and closer to the bridge, I started to second guess. Maybe I could switch lanes here and try my luck, trying to shake him through the city centre again. But again, back to my hunting ground, I knew every street, alley and shortcut there is - home ground advantage. I stayed in lane and we turned to go over the bridge, he was still a little bit back.

Then as I came over the bridge, I could see ahead the same kind of flashing lights approaching from the other side.

They were boxing me in.

I racked my brain for ideas in that split second to make a choice. I went with the only thing that made sense and gave me the best chance.

I braked sharply, sliding the car to a halt.

I stuffed the coke back into the bag and took the bag out with me. The police cars slid to a stop right in front of me, even mounting the footpath next to the road that I ran to. I kept running until I slammed into the wall of the bridge. I heard the car doors open and slam behind me and the cops shouting their instructions, telling me to stop and to get down.

I raised the bag up with my arm and threw it as hard as I could into the water below.

The next thing I could remember after the bag strap left my hand was the hard tackle to the ground and then the cold, rough, metal handcuffs being strapped onto me.

I only spent one night in the cell.

They never found the bag.

After what was initially disgust from Colin, turned to praise of a job well done. He also praised my quick thinking which immediately made me one of his go-to guys, instantly climbing the ladder in the pack.

After about a year and a half, we were getting into some deep feuds with rival gangs. We were only a small outfit. Colin was the one who held us together. The trouble we brought on the streets eventually started to follow me home. My relationship with my mum, dad and even Carl started to become tested.

We were eventually offered work down south, Dublin to be exact. I was twenty at the time.

Somehow our names had crossed conversations at the same table as Tommy Bray, the leader of one of the most feared gangs in Dublin.

He offered us a spot in the gang.

We couldn't turn down the opportunity, or the cash.

I stayed there for nearly five years.

The rest is history.

***

I drive myself and Carl to a small housing estate that has seen better days.

The houses need a big refurbishment, looking like they haven't changed or been touched since the seventies.

I drive deeper into the estate, past a bunch of rowdy teenagers by the side of the road who shout and bawl at the car as we pass. We take a turn into a cul de sac and I park outside one of the houses.

The houses we end up facing are very tidy compared to the rest of the estate, with green gardens, a small tree and flowers by the doors.

'Gimme the revolver,' I tell Carl.

He takes it out and hands it over to me. I hide it in an inside pocket of my leather jacket.

'It's not loaded. Did you grab the guns from my room?'

'Yeah but I don't need them right now,' I say.

'You're sure?' he asks.

'Wait here, I've got it,' I tell him,

I walk up to the house, following the path and keeping off the grass. I knock the door and look back at the car, waiting.

The door opens and I am greeted by a middle-aged woman in a flowery dress, with curly brown hair and a round face.

'Michael! Haven't seen you in a while, where have you been?' she asks smiling.

'Ah, I've been in hiding,' I joke.

'Colin will be so pleased to see you, it's been a while since you have come round.'

'He in?' I ask.

'Yeah, he's out the back, tinkering with his bikes as usual. C'mon in and I'll get him.'

She opens the door wider and I go inside. She leads me into the living room and offers me a seat in a large leather armchair, which I take.

'Do you want tea? Coffee?' she asks, her smile not shifting.

'No, thanks,' I say, smiling politely back.

'OK, I'll go get him.'

She leaves to get Colin and I take the time to look around the living room.

There is an old fireplace where they still burn coal and wood. The wallpaper is flowery which always reminded me of an older person's house, not something I thought Carl and his wife would have, he's only three years older than me.

Framed photographs of his children sit above the fireplace, on the mantelpiece.

Two daughters and a son from what I remember. Looks like the oldest daughter has left University, a graduation

180

photo takes the centre of the mantelpiece. I hear a door open and slam within the house, almost shaking it.

Thunderous footsteps get louder until Colin comes in from the kitchen.

'What the fuck are you doing here?' he blasts.

'You know why,' I tell him.

He steps closer.

'I want you the fuck out of my house, now!'

I stand up, preparing to defend myself.

'Not until I get a name.'

Colin's wife comes in.

'What's wrong?' she asks worryingly, her smile now absent, replaced by a look of confusion and fear.

'Nothing, Michael was just leaving,' Colin says.

'Names Colin, I just need one,' I tell him firmly.

Colin grabs me by the arm and tries to drag me towards the door.

'Get out!' he shouts in my face. I shrug off his hand and reach inside my jacket. Pulling out he revolver. Colin puts his hands up, submitting.

'Chill, Michael, chill.'

I walk towards him and he takes half a step back. I point the gun at him.

'Give me a name!' I shout.

'I can't, you know I can't!' he shouts back.

'Give me a fucking name!' I rage, raising the gun, putting closer into his face.

I back off, going over to the photographs on the mantelpiece.

'What if it was Sarah?' I ask, pointing at his daughter at her graduation.

'Don't,' Colin mutters.

'What would you do if it was her? Could you stop?'

'Please go, Michael. I don't want this to go any further.'

'It doesn't have to,' I tell him quietly.

Colin walks over and takes a seat in the armchair that I was sat in and looks at me bluntly.

'Let's get this over with,' he says.

He looks up at me, I leave the mantelpiece and walk over to him.

He raises his head up and closes his eyes.

I wait a moment for him to open his eyes.

I scramble my mind, trying to find the right words of interrogation or persuasion to get something from him but I know Colin, and I know he has a strong will. With his eyes still closed, I grab his wife and hold the gun to her head.

'Colin!' she cries.

Colin opens his eyes and once he sees the sight, he springs to his feet.

'Take that gun away from her head now!'

I don't utter a word, keeping my grip on his wife.

'Shaun Bray,' he says.

'Tommy's son?' I ask, a little surprised Tommy would send his own son to take Layla.

'Yeah, now let her go. You got what you came for.'

'I need a little more,' I say.

'Like what?'

'Where is he right now?'

'I don't know, but I know where he will be tonight.'

'Where?'

'He's going on a stag up in Belfast,'Colin says.

'I'll call in a couple of days for information. Information I can only get from you, and you better answer. If you tip them off that I'm coming or try to screw me over in any

182

way, I'll not come for you, or your wife. I'll come for Sarah,' I threaten.

'You fucking rat,' Colin scorns.

I let his wife run to the comfort of his arms.

I keep aiming at him until I leave the room, aiming with an empty gun.

I run out of the house, over the perfectly cut grass and into the car where Carl has taken the wheel for a quick getaway. We race out of the estate and out of Dublin.

***

We drive back to Belfast, back to our old hunting ground on the outskirts of the east of the city, the outer ring.

We park at the shops next to the large crossroads.

It's getting close to noon.

Without exchanging any words, we both make ourselves comfortable and fall asleep in the car.

'What now?' Carl asks.

I call Colin to get the name of the club. He tells me that Shaun is going to a nightclub called "Equinox" tonight. They'll likely be there after ten because they plan to go on a pub crawl beforehand.

I tell Carl who then slumps back in his seat.

'Great, just all day to wait,' he says.

We get lunch from the chip shop in the row of shops we are parked at. It's a long day of waiting. We spend it listening to the radio and planning tonight. Carl keeps raising doubts that we will get answers from Tommy's son, Shaun.

183

We get a taxi to the city centre at half nine.

The traffic is really starting to pick up at this time as everyone is on their way to the clubs of Belfast.

When we get into the city centre, the streets are packed with men and women, some rowdy, shouting and messing around on the way to their next destination. The rest of the people we see are already drunk, some even throwing up by the side of the road. We are taken into the Cathedral Quarter, the newly established hotspot in Belfast. It is filled with colour and lights draped along the fronts and sides of buildings.

The taxi takes us down the narrow streets of the quarter with people all around, inches away from the car as we try to creep our way through the crowds which also dominate the roads.

We get out on the next turn.

We quickly get swarmed by the crowd and get immersed in it.

Now to find the club.

I've never heard of it before. The last time I went for a night out in Belfast was about three years ago, everything has changed since then. We walk the footpaths and criss-cross the cobblestone road in search for the nightclub. Music echoes in the streets, almost as if it were playing through a series of wired-up speakers scattered throughout the area.

The bass of a song gets louder the further we walk in this direction. I spot start of the queue under the purple hue of light by the club entrance. I trace my eyes upward on the entrance to see the name of the club, "Equinox" - this is it.

I nudge Carl to look, we walk to the back of the queue and join it. The one thing I forgot about going clubbing and the one thing I didn't miss is the wait. The waiting in line, standing in the cold and, sometimes, wet streets. If it takes you any less than twenty minutes to get in at this time, you're doing great. Tonight, we don't have such luck. From the look of the crowd, it won't take that long, thankfully.

I'm hoping it's not all students in here. I don't fancy the idea of getting thrown up on by somebody who has just had their first-ever Jack Daniels because they want to impress their mates. We would stick out like a sore thumb too. It's like waiting in traffic, small gains every few minutes and people shouting from behind if you don't close that yard gap ahead of you the second it opens up.

I don't recognise anyone in the crowd.

'You're my eyes in here, I don't know what these guys look like,' Carl says.

'Just stay close to me, don't go wandering.'

We eventually get to the front of the queue where two large bouncers ask us for I.D.

They stand there studying them like we were trying to pass through customs.

Carl gets his I.D. back and is let inside. He waits inside the door for me but my bouncer must have difficulty reading, either that or he's being a deliberate asshole. Looking from my licence to me and then back again.

He finally lets me inside and we climb the stairs which have lights inside of them, up to the pumping music and dancing lights of the club above.

The first thing I notice is the ballet of movement on the dance floor, rhythmic dancing intertwined with bopping

185

heads sipping on drinks, and the shirtless rebels jumping up and down to the bass. I take the lead and push my way towards the bar.

I squeeze through the three-tier row of the queue, getting an elbow on the bar. After a few minutes, two people move and I get into eyeshot of the bartenders. Most of them are women, young student-types. One is a brunette with tied-back hair and heavy mascara with a smooth figure. She quickly disappears to the top of the bar, making way for her blonde colleague who eventually picks me out from the crowd.

'Yeah?' she asks, pointing to me and leaning her head in to hear my voice against the deafening music.

'Can I get two whiskey and cokes?' I shout to her.

She goes off to make the drinks and I look back over my shoulder to find Carl.

He's behind two guys right up my back. I reach out, grabbing his shirt and pulling him in next to me, past the two guys who make gestures and voice their frustrations.

I can't make out what they are saying but I ignore them, not wanting to make a scene. We get our drinks and start to make our way casually through the club.

Drinking as we go, after a few minutes, Carl leans into my ear when we stop at the other side of the dance floor.

'D'you see any of them?' he asks.

'No, not yet,' I tell him.

'You sure they haven't gone somewhere else? Maybe your guy has got it wrong.'

'Just give it a minute,' I insist.

We slowly start to push our way through the crowds again, even going out to the smoking area to scan around the faces.

The smoking area is up on the roof terrace of the club. A gap in between two buildings, complete with seating and tables.

There are even plant pots and a small wooden bar at the back. The wind blows in from the gap in the buildings above making it very cold. There are drops of water that remain on the varnished wooden tables. The droplets sitting there undisturbed from a previous short spell of rain.

'When is the last time you had one?' Carl asks, looking around at all of the smokers.

'I can't even remember. I might quit,' I say.

We leave the dim lights of the smoking area, swapping them for the dancing lights in the darkness of the club.

We walk over a patch of carpet that sticks to our shoes. I have to forcefully draw my feet up from the floor at points. I wonder what it is on the floor, is it just alcohol? But then I think it's best not to wonder. I've just finished my whiskey. I check Carl's which is still half full.

'You gonna drink that?' I joke.

'I am drinking it, you just downed yours when we were walking.'

'I'm gonna get another, what do you want?' I ask, drawing money from my pocket.

'Same again,' Carl says.

I ready the change from our last round, a couple of notes and coins, should be enough for another, even if the notes are just fives.

I weave my way into the queue at the bar again until I get stuck and can't go any further. I adjust my footing every few seconds to adjust my balance as people around me nudge into me or squash up closer for a better chance of getting to the bar first.

That's when I see him.

Through the shoulders and faces of the crowd, I see the smiling face of Shaun turning around from the bar with a handful of beers raised above his head and the crowd around him.

He has changed a little through the years but I still recognise his face from hanging around with Tommy. He used to be an errand boy. I push my way towards him, trying not to lose sight of him. He rejoins a group of guys, all in their early twenties, in tank tops and colourful t-shirts.

They all start to take beers out of Shaun's arms until they all have one each. Walking back into the club, I can't see Carl behind me as I follow them, I can't afford to wait for him, I can't lose Shaun, he'll have to come and find me.

Shaun and his friends retreat to a VIP table overlooking the dance floor in an area closed off by bouncers. I keep walking past as they go up the small set of steps to their table.

I take a stool at a table by a large pillar, just off from the VIP entrance. From here, I can still see Shaun and his friends. Now that they are seated, I get a better view of his pack. There are six of them altogether, including Shaun. All of his friends are quite tall and well built, it could be a fair fight with me and Carl. The only thing is the second we start trouble, the bouncers will break it up and we will be thrown out of the club and our chance will be gone. Shaun will have reinforcements called. I pick Carl out of the crowd as he walks past.

'Where the fuck did you disappear to?' he asks as he takes a stool next to me.

'Up there.'

He glances over his shoulder, staring intently for a moment before looking back at me.

'That cool crew?' he asks.

'Yea, Shaun is the guy in the red chequered shirt.'

'They're sitting comfortably up there.'

'Yeah, that's the VIP area,' I tell Carl.

'Might be here a while, I'm gonna go get them drinks you were meant to get,' he tells me, standing up.

'Here, you want this?' I ask him, offering him the handful of change I was going to use to get the drinks.

'It's OK, my round,' he tells me, patting me on the shoulder and leaving for the bar.

I don't take my eyes off Shaun and his group the whole time that Carl is away. People irritated me by getting in front of me, blocking my view, but all I could do is wait for them to move which they eventually did.

The other stools around me start to fill up and I do my best to keep Carl's stool free.

I leaned across the table over in front of Carl's stool so no one would want to sit there, maybe I looked really drunk too.

Carl comes back with the drinks, more whiskey and coke.

The night rolls on.

The rounds keep coming.

Carl gets every round so that I can keep an eye on Shaun to make sure he doesn't leave. He leaves the VIP area now and then.

He goes to the bar, the toilet and the dance floor. I never leave my stool to follow. I don't want to give myself away. He knows what I look like, he will know why I am here.

His time on the dance floor comes to an end after the biggest song of the night. I call it the biggest song because of the reaction of the crowd, everyone eats it up I can't help from tapping my hand on the table and rocking my foot on the stool rest.

Shaun and his pals go back to the VIP area again for the final part of the night, they bring a group of girls with them, too, to keep them occupied. I can't help but notice that Carl looks bored, barely touching his whiskey now.

I try to speak to him but the music has gotten so loud that I would need to get off my seat and take a step closer to him to speak.

I decide to leave it, focusing on my own drink, then I hear a voice in my ear.

'Hey there,' a soft, happy voice greets.

I turn to see two beautiful girls by my side, the closest, still leaned in to talk.

'What are ya drinking?' she asks.

'Whiskey tonight,' I tell her, raising my glass.

'I'm sorry, I had to come over. My friend here thinks you're cute.'

'No I don't!' her friends protests, laughing.

I look back up to the VIP area, they're still there.

'Do you want to buy us a drink?' the closest girl asks.

'No, thanks,' I tell them with my back to them.

'Pfft, fine whatever. You're very rude! You know that?' they shout as they walk around the back of my stool, past my line of sight.

They then swarm in on Carl who seems to perk up. He caters to them, flattering them. Soon they are sat beside Carl.

Carl must be using his arsenal of jokes and quips to keep them interested.

I sit through another three songs, one of which lasts several minutes. The club begins to empty out, getting close to that time, people must be thinking of leaving now to secure a taxi.

We remain though, just as Shaun does.

The crowd in the club starts to thin out, leaving us more exposed, I start considering moving to a different spot.

Then the bright white lights come on overhead and I hear a series of roars and shouting, Shaun and his friends have got to their feet, walking down from the VIP area to leave.

I get off my stool, waiting for Shaun to leave first. Carl is still in deep conversation with the two girls.

'Carl, hey,' I say, rocking his shoulder.

I walk ahead, hearing Carl stumbling off the stool behind me. I follow Shaun and his friends down the stairs and out into the wet and windy streets.

They don't hang around and swiftly make their way up the road.

I keep my distance, moving up along the crowds of the street behind them.

Carl catches up and starts walking alongside me.

'Any ideas yet?' he asks.

'Playing it as it comes right now,' I tell him.

We continue walking the long streets of Belfast city centre. Shaun and his friends make numerous bids for taxis but get turned away every time.

My clothes start to sag from their weight as the rain soaks them. My hands feel like ice in the breeze, with all attempts to dry them failing. They are all clearly drunk, staggering all over the footpath and messing with people along the way, either by shouting at them or bumping into them.

The footpath becomes clear ahead of them, apart from a young couple, a guy and his girlfriend walking slowly.

Shaun whispers something to his pals before walking a little ahead of them, walking in a collision course for the couple.

Shaun goes to the far side of the footpath where the girl is walking. He gets right up behind her and slaps her hard in the butt. Her knees buckled slightly from the force of the slap and Shaun jogs a little ahead of them, turning and laughing, taunting them.

The boyfriend lets go of his girlfriend's hand and confronts Shaun. Shaun puffs out his chest and squares up to the boyfriend.

The boyfriend punches Shaun, rocking him on his feet. He hits Shaun a couple of more times before Shaun gets a hold of him. Shaun's friends rush up to his aid and the odds play against the boyfriend as he is kicked and punched to the ground by the gang. The girlfriend tries in vain to make them stop. Once they do, she slaps Shaun across the face.

His face turns bright red, partly because of the slap and partly out of rage as he grabs her by the hair, yanking on it before pushing her backwards onto the pavement. It took a lot to not intervene but we can't mess this up.

Shaun's always been a scumbag, he doesn't have anything that resembles a conscience, a real rough cunt, just like Tommy.

Shaun and his friends stop outside a taxi depot.

Not wanting to get too close or run the risk by walking past them, we walk to the side of the road, pretending to hail a taxi.

There are three taxis parked, all of them have at least three people trying to reason with the drivers. We just stand back and watch it unfold, casually looking up the street now and then to check on Shaun.

Shaun and one of his friends go inside the depot.

The winds get rougher and the rain starts to lash down harder, a part of me wishes we were trying to hail a taxi for real.

Shaun emerges a few minutes later, the rain not letting up.

He pulls the collar of his shirt up around his neck for the little good it will do to keep him warm.

All of Shaun's friends start to walk into the depot for shelter but Shaun seems to be protesting. I can't make out what he is saying from here but there is a short conversation between him and two of his friends.

They nod, maybe in agreement or understanding as to what Shaun is saying and they go inside.

Shaun looks around the street and then goes to the side of the road.

I get back onto the footpath to get a better view. Shaun watches the heavy traffic passing by. As soon as there is a clearing, he runs across to the other side of the road. I go back to Carl.

'Hey, he's gone across the road,' I explain.

'OK, let's go.'

'Wait, you stay here in case he comes back across,' I say, grabbing his arm to halt him mid-walk.

'Do you know where he went?' Carl asks.

I look over to the taxis on the other side of the road. I can't make him out from the crowd, maybe he went into that bar? One last drink before the road.

But the further up the street I look, I find a narrow alleyway.

'I have an idea, wait here,' I tell Carl before crossing the busy road, weaving through passing traffic and almost getting clipped by the last car.

I get to the other side of the road and slow down to a steady walking pace again. I check the outside of the bar as I pass it but no one I can see is wearing a red chequered shirt. I continue up to the alleyway. I reach the entrance to it and look down. It's very dark and dingy, with multiple large bins scattered along it. I guess that they must belong to kitchens or restaurants.

I leave the busy and noisy street and descend into the quiet, murky alleyway. I walk even slower than I had on the street, almost like I were preparing for someone to jump out, or maybe I am.

The alleyway is completely empty, I can see the passing headlights of cars at the other end which looks to be at least a hundred yards ahead.

The trickling of water from the drainage pipes stands above the noise of the rain hitting the metal tops of the bins. I get about halfway down, the volume of bins has become denser.

They start to crowd up the alleyway, that's when I hear a kind of shuffling, mixed with the sound of a splashing puddle.

I duck down to the same height as the bins. I get up close to two bins merged together and peek my head up over the top, towards the source of the noise. I see the light brown hair of the back of Shaun's head.

When I stand up straight I can see that he is using the cover of the alleyway and the bins to take a leak.

I slowly move around the bins towards him, being careful with my footing as to not stand in a puddle and make any noise. I stop and duck down behind the last bin that separates me from Shaun.

I start to think about what I'm going to do, now or never, this is my chance, I won't get another when he leaves here. I stand up and walk around into plain view in front of him as he zips himself up.

'Fuck me mate, you scared the shit outta me,' he laughs as he struggles to adjust his trousers.

I freeze for a second, not saying anything, just staring at him.

He's so like Tommy it's uncanny, the voice, as well as the little gestures and body language.

He stares back at me, waiting for me to say something.

'Wait, I know you from somewhere. You used to work for my dad didn't you?' Shaun asks, studying my face well.

I maintain my silence, deciding my first move.

'Ah, OK. Well, gotta go,' he says, trying to walk past me but I push him back.

'What the fuck is your problem? ' he shouts, puffing his chest out.

He shrugs up his shoulders into a boxer's stance, weaving side to side, stepping towards me.

'C'mon then!' he shouts before throwing a wild swinging punch. I block the punch and pin him against the wall, throwing knees into his stomach before he slips onto the floor, cowering into a ball.

'What do you want? My wallet is in my back pocket, just take it and go,' he says.

'I don't want your wallet,' I tell him.

He studies my face as it comes into the glare of the light overhead.

'Michael?' he says, surprised. Finally pinning down exactly who I am.

'Where is she?' I demand.

'Listen, I ah—'

I drag him to sit upright.

'No messing around, no games. Where is my daughter?'

His look of shock and surprise slip off his face, a sinister and sickening smile takes its place.

'I said I wouldn't tell.'

He is his father's son. I know any line of questioning would lead to a dead-end but I had to try.

'Is she still alive?' I ask, trying to drag out any hints in his response.

'Go fuck yourself, you rat,' he says, smiling and then spitting into my face.

I stand up, wiping the spit off with the sleeve of my leather jacket.

'I need you to do me a favour,' I tell him.

'Oh, is that right?' he asks, smiling more widely.

'That's right,' I say, smiling back. 'Do you think he will get the message?'

'I don't know, maybe,' he says, resting his back against the wall, looking up at me laughing.

I laugh along with him, both our smiles broad. The smiles and laughter quickly disappear. Shaun leaps to his feet and I start backing off. He sprints at me as fast as he can and swings a punch. I duck under it and his momentum carries him on. He slips on the wet ground and falls face-first into one of the heavy metal bins.

The thud is sickening and he goes limp, laying on the ground with blood running from his head.

I kneel down to check his pulse.

He's gone.

'I think he'll get the message,' I mutter at Shaun's lifeless body.

I walk out of the alleyway and back across the road, back across to the line of taxis and Carl who is still amongst the queue.

'You find him?' Carl asks.

'Yeah.'

'And?'

'Went to plan. He's done. I need you to do something real quick.'

'What is it?'

'Tell his friends in the depot, you just saw some guy take a fall in the alleyway across the road. You saw him coming out from the depot and you want to know if anyone knows him.'

'Why? It's done. Let's not rock the boat.'

'We need them to find him, we can't let him lay to rot.'

'OK, I'm going,' Carl says reluctantly.

I stay within the taxi crowd and Carl walks up and disappears into the depot. Moments later, Shaun's friends come rushing out of it, running across the road and into the alleyway. Carl comes back down.

'Right, let's get the hell out of here,' he says.

We spend five minutes negotiating with a few taxi drivers until one offers to take us. We get in and get out of the city centre.

We are driving over the bridge, across the River Lagan and the shimmering lights of the tall buildings of the city disappear behind us. That's when the question comes.

'Where are you guys headed again?' the taxi driver asks.

I don't know what to reply with. My mind scrambles, trying to figure out somewhere to go, somewhere to retreat to.

There is nowhere; We have nowhere left, no place is safe. Where would the best place to be to wait this out? We are down to our last hundred pounds which rests in my pocket. That would maybe get a cheap hotel room for one night, but that's it. That's when Carl speaks up with an idea.

'Lisburn,' Carl answers. 'I'll give you directions when we get there.'

It's a long ride, the alcohol starts to takes its negative effect. My head starts spinning and aching.

The lights of cars and street lamps outside the taxi window start to blur and hurt my head.

We get to a small housing estate and Carl pays the fare.

We get out and I follow Carl up to the door of a small house.

He pulls his phone out and dials a number.

'Naomi, I need your help...yeah, come down, we are at the door. OK, bye.'

He hangs up and after a few moments, the green door unlocks and opens. Naomi appears from behind it in a black nightdress.

'Get in,' she whispers.

We go inside the house and she shuts the door behind us.

'You need a place to stay?' she asks, folding her arms and hunching her shoulders from the cold draft that we let in.

'Yeah, just for tonight,' Carl says.

I almost weigh in by saying a couple of nights but I resist, I am grateful for even one night with a roof over our heads.

'My mum is upstairs asleep. I don't think she would be too happy.'

'That's OK, we will find somewhere else,' Carl says.

Our hopes of a dry night fade until Naomi speaks again.

'My dad converted the shed out the back into a games room. There is a sofa bed in there. My mum never goes out to it. You can stay there as long as you want. I'll speak to her in the morning, she should be OK about that. You've met her before anyway,' she says to Carl.

'I know, she's lovely.'

'Well, I'm going back to bed. Just head on out through the back door. The shed will be open.'

'Thank you,' I tell her as she starts climbing the stairs again.

She ignores me, looking to Carl.

'We will be gone in a couple of days,' Carl says.

'Night,' she says and climbs the stairs, out of view.

She must still be feeling raw emotions from what has gone on.

We go out the back, down to the bottom of the garden and into the newly built, wooden shed.

Carl flicks on the light. This room has got it all. Pool table, a massive, wall-mounted flat-screen television, a sofa bed at the back of the room, which is already folded out into a bed, and a mini-fridge.

I start to wish I had this kind of room when I was younger. I go straight to the sofa bed, laying down in an attempt to get rid of my headache. Carl sets up the pool table and the balls.

'Fancy a game?' he asks.

I lay with my eyes closed, feeling a pounding in my head. A pool game is the last thing I want to do.

'Not a chance,' I mutter back.

'I'll play myself then,' Carl says, taking his first shot.

I hear the balls colliding and scattering around the table.

'You're used to playing with yourself anyway,' I joke, smiling to myself.

'Dick,' Carl mutters, taking another shot.

I hear him walking around the table, taking multiple shots as I try my best to drift off to sleep but my head won't allow it.

'You never told me your master plan. Are you gonna tell me?' Carl asks.

'Why we hunted down Shaun you mean?'

'Yeah. He didn't tell you where Layla is, did he?'

'No. Didn't expect him to.'

Carl stops playing.

'What do you mean?'

'He was never gonna tell me where Layla was. He was a stubborn son of a bitch.'

'Then what was the point of racing the whole way back to Belfast, to follow a stag night, knowing it was all for nothing?' he asks, irritated.

'Tommy isn't going to pop his head up above water for us to find him. We need a way to draw him out.'

'The funeral,' Carl catches on after a minute of thinking.

'He won't miss his own son's funeral. That's when we get the asshole.'

'If his son didn't talk, what makes you think Tommy will?'

'If I get hold of Tommy, I'll make him sing.'

200

DAY SEVEN

The next morning, Naomi brings breakfast out to us. Her mum helped her to make a fry up for both me and Carl. She actually engages in some small talk with me. Maybe she has forgiven my actions around her but I think it is more likely that she is trying to be civil.

She leaves me and Carl to breakfast. Once we are done, we walk down the road to the nearest bus stop and get a bus back to Belfast, to where we left the car.

When we step off the bus, we can't walk fast enough to where we left it, to see if it is still there.

Paranoia is pumping between us now, every car that slows down on the road, every horn, people shouting, it could be someone that is out for us. We make the walk up to the shops in good time. We keep our faces down when we wait at the traffic lights at the dual carriageway, again with the paranoia. We quickly look up and down the car park for Naomi's car. Carl spots the white bumper and leads us to it. He gets into the driver's seat whilst I go straight for the back seats, to see if our suits are still there.

They are still there, in their zip-bags.

I close the door, feeling a sense of relief. I get into the front.

I break a confession laying heavily on me to Carl.

'I need to make a stop seeing as we have time today.'

'Where? Where are you going?'

'To see Lisa, I'll need to take the car for a while.'

'Michael, fuck that, the bitch called the cops on you.'

'I need to see her, just for a little bit.'

'Do what you want, but I think you're stupid to go anywhere near her.'

'I'll drop you at Naomi's first,' I tell him.

'No, don't. I'll come with you and sit in the car. At least you'll have a quick getaway if she decides to Judas you again.'

I drive us up to Lisa's mother's house in Newtownabbey, just north of Belfast. We pull into the street and that's when I start having second thoughts. Is this a good idea? I don't even know what I hope to accomplish by seeing her. Maybe somewhere in the back of my mind, I think I can save our relationship.

I slow the car to a crawl, trying to buy myself a few more seconds to come up with what I am going to say to her when she opens that front door.

'You sure about this?' Carl asks, raising my doubts.

'Yeah,' I lie.

I pull us up outside her house and park. I turn the engine off and sit looking at the house in a sort of daydream. The house is bright white with large windows and a wooden gate at the side. The garden is well kept with a flower bed close to the house and a tidy but short wooden fence surrounding it.

'That the house?' Carl asks.

'Yeah, her mum's house.'

'Well, take whatever time you need. I'll park the car a little further down the street. Don't feel comfortable sitting outside that large living room window.'

I get out of the car and Carl shifts over into the driver's seat even before I get the chance to close the door. I open the small garden gate and walk carefully down the path to the front door, all the time I have an uneasy feeling that someone is watching me from behind the closed blinds of the house.

I knock three times and stand back from the door, not wanting to be too close to Lisa when she opens it. My nerves build with every second my knocks go unanswered until I hear the door opening.

The door swings gently inward and a pale, wrinkled woman stands behind it. It's Lisa's mum, Heather. She's never been a fan of mine. She always sneers at me, always a look of disgust on her face reserved for me.

'Can I see her?' I ask politely.

'What are you doing here?' she asks through her croaky voice.

'I want to talk to Lisa.'

'She doesn't want anything to do with you, whatever your name is.'

'It won't take long.'

I say that, knowing that it probably won't sway her but just then, Lisa appears in the hall behind her mum.

'It's OK mum,' she says, ushering her mum gently back inside.

'I just want a minute,' I tell Lisa.

'Get in,' she says after a moment of hesitation.

I follow Lisa down the hall, she closes the door of the living room shut as we head towards the kitchen. That must be where her mum has gone. We enter the kitchen and she shuts the door behind us.

'Please tell me what's going on,' Lisa pleads, her tone changing to a more desperate one.

'I don't know myself,' I tell her, trying to find a spot to stand in the kitchen.

'Do you know where she is?'

'Tommy has her.'

'And?'

'And, he wanted a hundred grand in cash for her.'

'Wanted? What do you mean wanted? That's past tense Michael.'

'I know. We met him. Me and Carl. We went down with the cash but Layla wasn't there.'

'Why? That was the deal so what was the problem? What did you do?'

'He said she became too hot to handle. Because the cops were involved and her face is all over the news.'

'Oh, god,' Lisa cries, her face becoming red.

'I wanted to wait until this is all over but I had to see you because there is a chance…'

'What do you mean? What chance?'

I stay silent. We both know what I meant.

'What chance, Michael?' she screams through the tears.

I go over to her and pull her close to my chest where she sobs even harder. At that moment, I remember what it was like before, holding her tight. Lisa lets go of me and starts pounding on my chest before she shoves me away.

'Get the fuck out of this house!' she shouts.

She turns and picks up a glass from the tabletop and throws it at me. It misses, smashing on the wall behind me.

'Get out!' she screams before sinking to the floor in a bed of tears. I leave the house as I hear the living room door creaking open.

I walk up the street to where Carl has parked the car and I get in.

'Ready?' Carl asks as he starts the engine.

I stay silent, ignoring him and gazing out the window in a daydream, trying to imagine how things would have been if our phone had never rung during that one dinner.

***

We park outside Naomi's house and Carl opens the door to get out.

'I'll be in soon, need to make a quick phone call,' I tell him.

'OK,' he says, getting out and closing the door.

I get out my phone and dial Colin's number. It's time. I hear it ringing.

'Hello, who is this?' Colin asks.

'It's Michael.'

'Michael...what have you done?'

'A son for a daughter,' I say coldly.

'You're gonna start a war here.'

'We're already at war.'

'What do you want?'

'You heard anything from Tommy?'

'They just got the body back.'

'Any word on the funeral?' I push.

'He's holding it early. He thinks you and that brother of yours will try and crash the funeral so he's going to have it tomorrow.'

'Where?'

'Michael, have some respect.'

'I'm far past respect for Tommy. Now, I know you don't want me to come to your house in the middle of the night so, where is he having the funeral?'

'You remember Father Kendal?'

'The anonymous drinking priest?'

'Yeah, used to always come into the local and the bartender always thought he was in fancy dress for a stag?'

'His church? The white one up the road from the local?'

'Yeah.'

'I'm guessing they will all be going to the local afterwards for a drink?'

'You know they will.'

'What time is the service?'

'Nine o'clock.'

'That's all I need to know, this is the last time you'll ever have to talk to me,' I say.

'So, we're done?' Colin asks.

'Yeah, we're done,' I tell him, hanging up the phone.

DAY EIGHT

We wake up to the deafening beeping of the alarm I set on my phone. It's six o'clock in the morning. We are both inside Naomi's shed sharing the fold-out bed.

We immediately get changed into our suits and do our hair. As we both check and adjust ourselves in front of the large mirror in the room, Naomi walks in. She is still in her nightgown with a robe wrapped around her.

'What are you doing up this early?' she asks.

'We need to leave early today,' Carl explains.

'You both look like you are going to a funeral,' she says.

Me and Carl look at each other, understanding the irony of her statement.

'When will you be back?' Naomi asks.

'I don't know,' Carl tells her as I go to the sofa bed to pick up my blazer.

'I'll call you, OK?' Carl continues, putting his arms on Naomi's shoulders, embracing her.

'We've gotta go, now,' I tell Carl, throwing on my blazer.

Carl looks to me and nods before looking back upon Naomi. I walk past him and out the door. I'll wait in the car while they say their goodbyes again.

It's another five long minutes before Carl comes out from the side of the house.

He adjusts his collar and then his cufflinks. He gets in the passenger seat.

'You ready?' I ask him.

'Yeah let's go.'

'You don't have to come, you know that? You've done enough.'

'I've done enough whenever Layla is home,' he tells me, staring into my eyes, his gaze unflinching.

I nod, out of agreement and thanks.

I start up the car and we start the drive.

***

We get to Dublin just before eight o'clock.

Something feels different in the air, a tension.

We get to Tommy's housing estate, an estate I used to know all too well. The footpaths are all filled with parked cars and there is a police presence. Two squad cars sit on the corner of Tommy's street. Further on down the road, a large crowd has gathered, mostly donned in black suits. I continue, driving down the next street in search of a parking space.

I find a gap between two cars halfway down the road and struggle to get the car parked in the tight space. We are still early, they won't be leaving the house for almost another hour. I switch off the engine and radio and lie back in my seat.

'What now?' Carl asks.

'We're early, we need to just wait until they head to the church and we'll follow.'

We wait for a while until we see the large convoy of cars leaving the estate, following a hearse. We mix in and follow the convoy to a church in the centre of Dublin.

We watch the funeral car the whole way, trying our best to not get mixed up with different flows of traffic. I keep an eye on the road as well as the cars around us. Enemies to our front, enemies at our backs. I watch the eyes of the drivers at our backs for anything out of the ordinary. To our front, I only pray that those in the back seats of the cars keep their attention forward.

The convoy arrives at the church and turns into the grounds.

We continue straight, avoiding going into the lion's den.

It's safer to wait out here.

I park up.

'OK, we going or what?' Carl asks, reaching for the door handle.

'No, wait,' I tell him, putting my hand out. 'Now isn't the time.'

'So, when is the time?' Carl asks, slumping back in his seat, disappointed.

'We'll get him when he comes out and goes to the bar.'

'What bar?' Carl asks.

'The same bar he goes to after every funeral.'

'I don't know if you're ballsy or just bat-shit crazy,' Carl tells me, smiling in disbelief.

'Yeah, well. Maybe a bit of both. You're the one who wanted to go in there to try our luck.'

'Fair point but less chance of seeing us coming. Lots of places to hide.'

'Like where? The fucking confession box?' I joke.

'Fine, we're doing it you're way aren't we? I'm fucking sick of sitting in this car.'

I turn up the radio as Carl continues to rant, blocking him out and watching the church.

I keep skipping the radio stations to find something that isn't a brainless pop song by some pretty karaoke singer who can't write her own songs and sells most of their records based on how she looks. Too many to name. I land on the flip-side of the coin, country singers singing about their sweetheart who stole their truck...there's just no winning.

I turn it off and start to play a game with time. I look away for what I think feels like five minutes and turn back to see if I am right. Most of the time only two minutes had passed.

My patience starts to thin.

I eventually stop watching the time as it's only making it drag out longer. I start staring at a flock of pigeons on the footpath, refusing to even move for people walking past, fighting over the remains of someone's early morning fry from a local chip shop. They start to get defensive of their fry, flapping their wings at a group of women walking too close to it.

We sit through numerous chimes of the church bell and then the mourners and the wash of black and white, floods out of the church and into the large front car park. I look intensely through the crowd, trying to find Tommy but there are so many people here and it's hard to pick one man out from the vast swarm that are getting close to the front gates.

'See him?' Carl asks.

'Not yet, can barely make out the faces from over here.'

'You think they will going to that bar yet?'

I take another final look around the crowd as they start to empty out on to the street. I look away in fear of being spotted and turn back to Carl.

'Let them get down there ahead of us and then we'll head down.'

'OK,' Carl says, shifting a little in his seat as mourners start walking past the window of the car.

We wait until the road becomes empty and all of the cars parked around us start up and leave until we are one of the only cars left.

'OK, let's go,' I say, starting up the engine.

I drive us a short journey down the main road and through a couple of side streets until we start seeing the row upon row of parked cars filling each side of the road.

I start to slow down, knowing the bar is at the corner of the street ahead.

'We here?' Carl asks.

'Yeah, it's on the corner up there.'

I find a space between the cars and squeeze the car into the space.

I get out and open up the boot, I open the bag with the pistol and the rifle in it. I take the pistol and stuff it into my blazer before going back to speak to Carl.

'I take it I'm sitting this one out?' he asks, annoyed.

'If it goes south in there, I need to know Layla still has a chance beyond me.'

'Make sure she doesn't have to,' he tells me.

I close my door, watching Carl slide over into the driver's seat.

He puts down the window.

'If I manage to pull this off, odds are, we are gonna have to get out of here in a hurry,' I tell him.

'Got it,' Carl says confidently.

I open my mouth to speak, to say something, something like, goodbye, thanks, something like that. I think Carl senses it.

'Forget it, just get in there and get back out here,' he tells me firmly.

I walk away without another word. My focus ahead, ahead at the noisy bar on the corner.

I enter the bar to the sound of singing and the chatter of the mourners.

It is an old-fashioned bar.

Dark wooden furnishings and even glass ashtrays on the tables. Above the bar is where an Irish flag is nailed, along with old newspaper headlines that have been framed.

Among the many men of all ages crammed in here, there are also women and children sat amongst the spaced out wooden tables and chairs. The windows are dirty and full of the remains of ripped off posters and stickers. The glass is not the common see-through panes but rather a distorted, thick glass.

I try to blend in, going straight to the bar to order a drink.

The air is thick with cigarette smoke and the smell of the dark wood. As I wait for my drink I look around for Tommy or any familiar faces that could expose me.

I find Tommy at the other end of the bar, at a table with his family.

I remember his wife's face and the small boy beside him is his other son Robert, he must be around fifteen by now.

When my drink arrives I decide to stay at the bar, using the small crowds around me to obstruct Tommy's view. He won't spot me from here but I can watch him. Upon further scanning of the room, I recognise a few other guys, old gang members, but they are too preoccupied by the company they have to take any notice of my gazes.

I'm halfway through my pint when drunks stumble into me from the side. They start shouting at the bartender as they hang on to each other around the shoulders. The small crowds around me start to leave and go to grab tables, leaving me out in open view of the bar.

I keep the pint glass to my face, pretending to drink it as I walk away from the scene that the drunks have caused in the bar. All eyes are on them as I try to find a space to retreat to.

I find a space against the wall where those who didn't get seats are standing.

Again, I try to blend in by making it appear that I am part of a group but excluded from the conversation.

I keep carefully checking around to look at Tommy.

I feel the handle of the pistol inside my blazer, checking it is still there. I start to dwell on the thought of just rushing Tommy in front of everyone, drawing the gun to his head and getting answers.

But even if I did get the answers I wanted, there would be no way I'd ever leave this place. It would be a death sentence.

I start to get comfortable in this awkward situation. Confident that no one notices me, I go to the bar for another round. I get another pint glass of beer and start sipping the foam at the bar when I hear a familiar voice almost next to me.

It's Tommy, two men stand between us at the bar, the closest we've been since the carnival.

'Alright Gerry,' he greets the bartender.

'What can I get ya, Tommy?'

'Give us four pints of Guinness,' he says.

'We've just ran out. I need to get a new barrel from the back.'

'It's OK, I'll get it,' Tommy suggests.

'Nah Tommy, don't worry about it,' the bartender says.

'No, it's OK. You're off your feet today with this lot. Let me go grab it for you.'

'Thanks, mate,' the bartender says, taking a new order from a group further up the bar.

I bow my head as Tommy comes around the back of me.

I watch him out of the corner of my eye, going through a door marked "Staff only". I wait a few seconds after the door closes and leave the bar, walking casually after him.

With a last check to see if anybody is watching, I quickly go in through the door after Tommy.

I walk through a small cold corridor. Empty beer boxes lie on the ground at the sides of the corridor. The corridor opens up into a small back room with a shutter door.

There are stacks of crates that take up much of the room, with beer barrels lining the stone wall beside the shutter. I hear something drop and roll along the ground.

I carefully edge around the crates to see Tommy leant over, removing boxes from on top of a beer barrel.

'Fuck,' Tommy mutters as bottles fall out the bottom of one of the boxes he lifts, smashing at his feet.

I step out into plain sight behind him.

He notices my footsteps and turns around, stumbling back in surprise.

'What the fuck are you doing here?' he asks.

I pull out the pistol from my blazer and take aim.

Tommy stumbles and falls, moving further and further backwards, trying to avoid the sight of the gun gripped hard in my hand. I walk him down until he backs up against a wall.

214

'Where is she?' I shout.

'I'll let you walk away. Put that gun away, turn around and walk out.'

I grab him by the collar and pistol whip him in the face until he drops to the ground.

I kick and stomp on him as hard as I can.

When I stop, he starts to cough on the ground, spitting out blood too. I pick him up off the floor and push him back against the wall. I step right up to him, pushing the barrel of the gun into his cheek.

'You killed Shaun, didn't you? You bastard!' he shouts.

'I'm not walking away from anything. Is she still alive?'

He says nothing so I push the barrel harder into his cheek.

'Is she?'

'I don't know,' Tommy replies reluctantly.

'Where is she? Where are you keeping her?'

'I don't have her.'

'What do you mean you don't have her?'

'You stupid fuck, you got the cops involved. She was too hot to handle, we had to pass her off.'

'To who?'

'I can't say,' Tommy says.

'You can't say or you won't?'

'There a difference?' he asks smugly.

'I'll walk back through that door and spray shots all around that bar. I don't care any more, I really don't. Your wife, she's back there isn't she? And your son, Robert,' I say, pointing with the gun towards the direction of the bar.

'You're a piece of work, Michael.'

'I can't promise you'll walk out of here. But if you tell me, you have my word your family will be safe,' I tell him.

Tommy takes a deep breath, looking around.

'I sold her to Bulgarians,' he tells me.

'What? What Bulgarians?'

'They buy and sell people. We use some of their girls for the club.'

'You sick fuck,' I say with gritted teeth, wanting to knock his crooked ones in.

'Gotta do what ya gotta do in these circumstances,' he says coldly.

'Where can I find them?'

I start to lower my gun when Tommy suddenly reaches for something inside his blazer.

I shoot.

I shoot him twice in the chest, he slumps back against the wall and slides to the floor, gasping for air.

I walk over to him and throw open his blazer to reveal the blood-stained white shirt.

Tucked into his belt I find what he was reaching for, a small revolver.

He looks up at me, through the gasps for air, he smiles, showing his blood-stained teeth.

'Heh, heh, god knows what they've done with your little girl,' he says.

'Where can I find them?'

He starts to cough violently, gasping more desperately for air. I kneel down to comfort him long enough to get an answer.

'Where are they?'

A final, single breath escapes Tommy.

He's gone.

I look around sharply, the room is still empty. I take one last look at Tommy, the catalyst of this whole thing. Even with his death, it's still not over. I tuck away my pistol and leave through a fire door.

I come out onto a narrow alleyway.

I run down the alley and around to the front of the bar where Carl is still waiting in the car.

I get into the passenger seat, startling him from his daydream.

'Get us out of here,' I tell him.

He drives us away from the bar.

'What happened in there?' Carl asks.

'We need to go down to the old club,' I tell him.

'What about Tommy?'

'He's done, I clipped him in the back room.'

'Where's this club? What's there?'

'Keep straight here. I need to find someone I used to know. I think she still works there.'

'What's going on?' he asks.

'They don't have Layla.'

'What do you mean? Of course, they do.'

'They sold her.'

'Sold her? To who?'

'That's what I'm about to find out,' I tell him confidently.

I guide Carl through the busy streets of Dublin, to up the north of Dublin to an area called Swords. I lean forward in my seat, looking past Carl as we pass a club with two large bouncers outside and glittering lights coming from inside the large double doors.

Carl notices me looking.

'What? Is that the place?' he asks, looking back.

'Yeah, it looks different. I don't remember it looking so...up market.'

I ask Carl to park two doors up.

I take out the pistol I finished off Tommy with and hand it over to Carl.

'Can't get in carrying, hold on to it for me.'

'You making me babysit the car again? Are they not gonna recognise you?'

'Let's hope not,' I say with a careless smile before shutting the door on my way out.

I straighten my clothes and ruffle my hair into some sort of shape on my way up to the two massive bouncers stood outside the club.

I walk in the middle of the two bouncers, bound for the opened doors of the club when a large, hairy arm comes out in front of me. I look up at the two towering bouncers that look down at me like a school kid.

'Can we help you, buddy?'

'Yeah, you can move that hand before I move it for ya,' I tell him firmly.

'Piss off,' he tells me.

I see his friend on my left shuffling into position to strike so I take half a step back.

'I've business inside. You want me to tell Tommy you turned me away, on today of all days?'

They both look at each other, everyone always shit themselves on the sound of Tommy's name.

'Go on,' they both say. I walk past them and into the club.

I enter the darkness of the club to the repetitious music. It is sparsely occupied.

Customers are scattered around the various tables and chairs within the club, some around the dancing poles,

218

some off watching from a distance and others at the stools of the bar.

It's a strip club.

There are only a few girls dancing on the poles in their underwear. Even the waitresses dress provocatively in corsets and stockings.

The whole club was a vision of Tommy's, in the pipeline for years. He finally set it up, not long after Colin brought me down south. I'm on a search as I walk deeper into the club. I'm looking for a girl, I'm looking for Roxy.

I go to the bar and grab the bartender's attention from the edge of the bar. 'Hey, does Roxy still work here?' I ask.

'Roxy? Yeah, she's working now,' the bartender says.

I look around at the girls dancing, none of them is Roxy.

'She out back?' I ask, pointing to a curtain at the side of the large stage at the back of the club.

'Must be, probably out having a cigarette. If you're going out to see her, tell her to get her ass back in here will ya? Would just take for Tommy or one of the managers to walk in and then bust all of our balls over it.

'Yeah, sure,' I tell him, leaving for the curtain.

I get backstage and find my way out the back of the building, it all comes back to me as I walk, I remember what doors to take.

When I get out the back of the building, I find a woman standing by the bins. I walk over, calling out Roxy's name.

It is Roxy, she turns around as I walk over to her and she looks the same as the day that I left on the drug run. We used to be a thing, me and Roxy. An on and off thing to be honest, but I always cared about her. She still has that jet black hair that curls the whole way down to her shoulders.

219

'Michael? Michael…what the fuck are you doing here?' she shouts, stubbing out her cigarette on the bin next to her.

'I need your help,' I admit.

'No, you need to get out of here before Tommy finds out you're here.'

'It's OK, don't worry about me, I need to know something.'

'What?' she asks.

At that moment, the back door of the club swings open and two other girls come out to light up cigarettes. They stop and stare at us staring back at them.

'C'mon,' Roxy insists, grabbing my arm and dragging me back into the club. She takes me into an empty room and closes the door.

'Right, what is it?' she asks.

'Where does Tommy get his new girls?'

She sighs and a glum look comes across her face. She takes out another cigarette and takes a seat on the black leather sofa in the room. I turn around to see what it is facing. On the other wall, a large glass panel, peering into another small room that is covered in red upholstery.

This is a private showroom.

'Why do you want to know that? They aren't the kind of guys you want to run into.'

'They have my daughter.'

Roxy gasps and then starts to bite her nails, a worried look on her face. She seems to be thinking, maybe of something positive or optimistic to raise my spirits.

'Just tell me where to find them,' I tell her.

'I went the first time, along with Tommy. He wanted me to help pick them.'

Roxy goes on to tell me every detail of how they came to get some of the girls working at the club now. She tells me everything I need to know.

Not long after I leave the club, me and Carl pull up on a flea market in the backfield of a church, just south of Dublin.

We get out and I take lead, looking out for a tent that Roxy mentioned.

It's a small tent, somewhere on the outskirts of the market with dragon designs on it.

We pass from each side of the market to the next in search for it.

People are selling all sorts here. From old computer games, rugs, pottery, to beaten up furniture and artwork.

We've searched almost every corner of the market when I spot a red tent in the distance.

On the side of it, I see the head of a dragon on it, it must be it. I hasten my walk, taking Carl by surprise who jogs to catch up.

Outside the front of the tent is a tall, bearded man with a small stall in front of him with numerous fishing accessories on it and rods laid on the grass at the foot of it. I walk casually up to him and greet him.

'Hi, I was wanting to know what you have for sale.'

'Just what you see, my friend,' he says, he has a foreign accent.

'I was hoping to see what you've already caught,' I tell him.

Roxy told me that this is the phrase that Tommy used to gain access to the tent. She didn't tell me what I would find inside though.

The man looks at me strangely after saying it.

221

'Who are you? I don't know you,' he says.

'You had recent business with my employer. Local guy, Tommy? He was here only last month. He liked what he got, wants to know if you've got any more?'

'No, no, I'm sorry. We are out of stock.'

'What's in the tent?' I ask.

'None of your concern,' he says firmly.

Carl makes the first move, grabbing him by the throat and knocking over his stall. I go past them and straight into the tent.

Inside I see two posts hammered into the ground, numerous lines of cord are tied and stretched between them. Pegged to the cords are small, hand-cut photographs. Photographs of young kids.

They are all amateur mug shots, the children are all stood in front of the same wall which has old styled wallpaper with numerous tears in it. The children look sad and neglected. I start from one end and work my way quickly to the other, trying to find Layla. I make the trip two or three times, still not being able to find her when Carl comes inside with a strong grip on the merchant.

'Where are these kids?' I ask angrily.

The merchant's expression is blank.

I take one of the photographs off the line and shove it into the merchant's face.

'Where are they?' I shout at the height of my voice.

I take the pistol off Carl and point it in the merchant's face.

That's when the fear pours out and he slowly descends to his knees, begging.

'Please, please, please,' he pleads on the brink of tears.

'Where are they?' I shout again.

'I take you there, I take you there now.'

'OK, take us there,' I say, putting the gun away.

Carl hoists the merchant to his feet and we all leave the tent together. Carl leads the way back to the car, ushering the merchant with a strong grip on his arm. I fall back to walk behind them in case this guy gets any ideas.

***

The merchant gives Carl directions out of Dublin, the whole way to an old beaten-up country road when we start to slow down. There are mostly fields either side with some derelict old houses that are falling apart. The rain has started to come on heavy.

'Just up this road now,' the merchant says.

Carl slams on the breaks, surprising us all.

He gets out of the car and then opens the back door, dragging the merchant out of the car.

'Now get the fuck out of here or I'll kill you myself!' he shouts.

I turn in my seat to see the merchant running back down the road.

Carl gets back in and resumes driving.

About halfway up the road, I spot a large barn on the left-hand side. Beside it is a small white farmhouse. This must be it. I tell Carl to turn down into the road.

The road is very rocky.

We come to a stop right outside the farmhouse.

I check the magazine of the pistol and slide it back in.

'Stay here,' I tell Carl.

'Again?' he asks, annoyed.

'There's a rifle in the boot, I might need that back up this time,' I admit.

I get out of the car and walk up to the front door.

I knock and wait for an answer.

The whole place looks dated, the stone covered road even leading up here is full of potholes which have turned into large puddles.

Moss and weeds have started to reclaim most of the path as well as the house.

A large barn across from us looks rusted and ruined. I can even see the imperfections in its metal frame and gaps in the roofing.

I hear the door unlock and a tall skinny man with a thick, black beard answers.

He speaks in a foreign language, it's phrased as a question, I know that much.

'I'm here to buy. Tommy Bray sent me, we are looking more girls for the club.'

He speaks again in a strange language and holds up his hand as a gesture I take as wait. He disappears into the house, leaving the door slightly ajar.

Moments later, another man appears at the door, an English speaker.

He is in his mid-twenties like the first guy, also with a black beard.

'Can I help you?' he asks with an accent.

'I'm here on behalf of Tommy Bray. We've done business before, we are looking to buy more girls for the club.'

'Come inside, please. Novak is in the kitchen, you speak with him.'

The man opens the door wide and I go inside. He shuts the door behind us and escorts me to the kitchen.

The house has a really bad damp smell and most of the wallpaper is peeling off the walls.

The floor is littered with all kinds of rubbish, most of it trampled into the carpet.

We enter the kitchen where four men are sat around a small wooden table, playing cards.

We stop by the doorway and I wait for the guy to say something or introduce me but he stays silent. The men at the table take no notice of us and continue to play. I break the silence, interrupting the card game.

'Who is Novak?'

They all stop playing and look up at me. One of them speaks up, a man with black slicked-back hair and a spider tattoo on his forearm.

'I am Novak,' he says.

'I'm here on behalf of Tommy Bray. We are looking to buy.'

'Sorry but we have none for sale,' he says.

'You're saying you can't even find a couple of girls for us? I have the cash in the car.'

'Did you not hear me? The stock we have in the barn is going on the bus tomorrow. They're all bought and paid for.'

The barn. So that's where they are.

'What was their price? I'll guarantee to beat it,' I tell Novak.

'It's not up for discussion,' he tells me sharply.

I walk around the table and pull a chair up beside Novak and sit down beside him as the other men adjust in their seats, waiting to strike.

'When will you have a new batch in?'

'One month.'

'I don't know much about this business. Aside from the girls for the club, I was looking for some for myself.'

'Not a problem, my friend.'

'These girls are they, I mean. Have they been around the block? Are they hooked on anything?'

'No, all girls are pure and we don't use the drugs on them. Devalues the girls, lowers the price.'

'Ah, I see. What price would we be talking?'

'Come back next month and we will discuss prices. Now please, we are trying to play a game here.'

My English speaking escort comes around the table and stands over me. 'Time to go,' he says.

I keep my eyes fixed on Novak but he turns away and starts to play cards again.

My escort drags me up to my feet by my arm.

Once on my feet, I shrug him off, spin around him and take his back, my arm around his neck.

I take out the pistol with my other hand and start shooting the players at the table.

They all start diving to the floor, I shoot two of them dead in their chairs. More men come in through the kitchen door with guns. They shoot but hit the escort, my shield, and I return fire, gunning them down. Novak crawls under the table as I take cover behind the kitchen cabinets near the back door. More and more men enter the room shooting.

I'm pinned.

Then I hear automatic fire rattling through the house. I pop out from cover and shoot the last of the men standing in the kitchen, distracted by the distant gunfire. The whole kitchen is a mess of bodies and blood.

I hear the whimpers of Novak under the table.

There are footsteps approaching from the hallway.

I take aim at the door and see Carl poking his head in with a rifle in his hands.

He must've got it out of the boot in a hurry.

'Michael! You OK?' he calls.

'All clear!' I answer back.

Carl steps into the room. I throw the pistol on the kitchen floor and flip up the wooden table to reveal Novak.

'Where is the little girl?' I shout.

'What little girl?' he asks panicked.

'The little girl Tommy Bray sold to you, the Irish fella.'

'I don't know, we have lots of girls that come and go through here. I don't deal with everyone.'

'Are there girls in that barn outside?'

'Yes, yes!'

I leave him laying on the floor and walk past Carl, out into the hallway.

I hear Novak's cries before the sound of Carl's gun going off.

I leave the house and run across to the barn, through the heavy rain and over the stone covered ground.

I reach the door of the barn and push open the large, heavy, rusted door. It creaks loudly as it swings inward.

The ground is covered in mud and hay. There are empty stables the whole length of the barn on my right, on my left is a series of rag covered structures that look like large boxes or crates.

The rain rattles heavily on the steel sheeted frame of the barn, some of the rain dropping right through the gaps in the roof and creating puddles in exposed areas. I go up to the closest rag and pull it off.

I almost freeze in shock with what is revealed underneath.

Heavy-duty steel barring of a cage, the cage door has a large padlock on it and inside, there is a person.

What looks to be a woman in her early twenties, her clothes are dirty and ripped, her face is covered by a rag which has a slot cut for where her mouth is. Beside her is a worn-out blanket and a bowl of water, the kind of bowl you would give to a dog.

I hear the creak of the barn door and turn to see Carl enter.

He stops on the spot, taking in what I've just seen.

I go to the next rag, I pull it down and I see the same thing, another girl, dirty clothes, blanket and rag over her head.

'Who is it? Please, let me go. I wanna go home, I wanna go home!' she burst out shouting.

I go to the next rag and then the next and the next. The barn is now full of women screaming for their freedom, but I have not found Layla yet.

I pull the rag off one of the last cages to reveal a small girl. She's laying face down and not moving.

Those pyjamas, they're the same as Layla's. I try to contain my excitement at the prospect of actually finding her and try to find a way of breaking the lock.

I look around and find a shovel laid against one of the empty stable doors.

I grab it and come back to the lock. I lift the shovel up and start driving it down on the lock as hard as I can.

Over and over I chop at it until it finally breaks. I scramble to unlock the cage and I go to the small girl inside.

Carl comes to the doorway of the cage as I lift the girl off the ground and into my arms.

I undo the rag covering her face and take it off.

Her eyes are shut, her lips are dry but I hear faint breathing.

Her eyes start to open, them same brown eyes I've known since the day she was born, her mother's eyes.

'Layla,' I whisper, my throat getting tight and my eyes start to water.

'Daddy?' she says.

Her eyes widen more and she bursts into life, grabbing me around the neck and gripping on tight. She starts to sob into my shoulder.

'It's OK, I'm here. I'm taking you home.' I lift her up and carry her out of the cage. Carl leans in to look at her.

'She OK?' he asks.

'Yeah, I need to take her home.'

'What about the people in here?' Carl asks.

'Break them out, call the police to come out here.'

'What? Are you nuts?'

'They're after me, they're not after you. We can't leave these people alone.'

'OK, what about the guys in the house?'

'Tell them it was me. Tell them I got my daughter back. When you start hearing the sirens, get rid of that,' I tell Carl, looking at his gun.

'I will don't worry.'

'Thanks, for everything,' I tell him with tears coming down my face.

'Sure, no problem. What's family for eh?' he says, smiling, on the verge of tears himself.

I wrap my free arm around him, embracing him tightly, I feel his tight grip around me too.

'Now, go on. Get outta here,' Carl says with a smile.

I take Layla out to the car and place her in the back seat.

I get in and drive out of the farm.

***

We have just re-entered Northern Ireland and I look into the back seat to check on Layla, she is asleep. I start to ponder on my next move. Where do I go from here?

I have nowhere to take her to. I have nowhere to go to myself. Tommy might be dead but I will still have a lot of enemies looking to get even.

I take my phone out and ring the city airport in Belfast. I order a last-minute flight for myself to Scotland. I have some family there, we haven't spoken in years but we are still on good terms, it's the only thing I can think of. The person on the other end of the line tells me that I will be able to collect my last-minute ticket when I arrive at the airport.

I can't take Layla with me. It's not where she belongs, she belongs at home. That's why I am taking her there.

We drive the whole way to Glengormley, to her granny's house, Lisa's mothers.

When I pull into the street, I check back again to see that Layla is still asleep and I carefully park up outside of Lisa's mother's and turn off the engine.

230

I look at the house and see Lisa come to the window and spot me. Although I can't hear her, I can see that she is shouting and pointing at me, her old mum appears alongside her, listening to Lisa's protest.

I get out of the car and before I can open the back seat door, Lisa comes storming out of the house, shouting at me.

'What the fuck are you doing here? I want nothing more to do with you! Who the hell do you think you are?'

'Lisa, just wait a minute,' I say, trying to calm her down.

She gets right up in my face. 'The cops are on their way, get out of here and stay out of my life. You've ruined my life.'

She continues her attack of words and I realise nothing I say is going to calm her down or stop her, so, amidst her abuse, I reach for the door handle of the back seat and open it.

Lisa looks inside to see Layla and falls silent. She slowly reaches into the back seat, sweeping Layla's hair from her face and hugging her tight, waking her up.

'Mummy!' I hear her cry.

Lisa emerges from the back seat as does Layla. Lisa falls to her knees on the pavement, hugging Layla more intensely as they both sob. Lisa looks up at me from over Layla's shoulder.

'Thank you! Thank you! Thank you!' she says to me.

I see Lisa's mum appear at the front door of the house, her hand covers her mouth as she spots Lisa holding Layla.

Lisa lets go of Layla.

'Go to your granny for a minute, honey,' Lisa tells her.

'What about Daddy?' she asks, looking up at me.

'C' mere,' I say softly to her.

I drop to my knees as she runs into my arms. I hug her tightly and kiss her on the cheek.

231

'I love you. Now go to your granny, go on.'

I let her go, wiping the tears from both her eyes and my own. She runs off over to Heather.

Lisa walks up to me.

'I have to go, I can't stay,' I tell her.

'Where are you going?'

'I can't say.'

'Will we see you again?'

'Hard to say. I hope so,' I say, trying to force a smile but my emotions get the better of me and my lower lip trembles.

Lisa throws her arms around me, holding me tight.

'Thank you for bringing her back to me, Michael.'

I start to hear the distant sound of sirens and Lisa lets go.

I get back into the car with everybody watching. Lisa goes back to the house, they all stand watching me from the front door. I wave my last goodbye and move off down the street.

I race through the streets and back down the motorway. I need to go back to the house one last time.

I need to get that passport.

I drive back to Holywood.

I pull up outside my old house and rush inside. I go straight upstairs and under my bed and pull out a plastic box filled with junk. I take off the lid and toss it away, searching and scattering my way through old letters, certificates and other bits of paper towards the bottom of the box.

I find old phones, pens and tangled wires at the bottom but still no sign of the passport. I lift the box, tipping its contents onto the carpet and spreading it all out to get a better look. There it is plain as day. I snatch up my passport and put it into my back pocket and leave the mess on the floor. I run out of the room, down the stairs and out through the open front door of the house.

I look up and down the street on my way back to the car and notice a dark grey car creeping down from the corner of the street. I get into the car and reverse back out onto the road. I keep a casual driving style the whole way out of the area while the grey car tails me.

I get to a give way sign and wait for traffic to ease so I can move out. I turn on the radio and put it up loud, listening to the presenter.

'Now it's time for the listener's request and we have a great choice here that comes in from David in Belfast. He's looking for a classic from the late seventies, well, here you go David. Live, on radio 7.'

I smile as the guitar riff starts and I turn it up louder. I put it into first as soon as the blue flashing lights illuminate on the grey car, an undercover.

I slam on the accelerator and take off, the undercover car speeds up right behind me. I take the narrow residential street corners at twice the normal speed, trying to outpace the undercover car but it keeps right on me. I've driven through these streets long enough to know where I can take corners fast and where to go slow.

I leave Holywood swiftly, getting onto the dual carriageway, bound for the airport. Soon, a marked police car joins in the chase behind me alongside the grey undercover car. They keep a tight gap behind me. We speed the whole way back towards Belfast.

I dance my hands along with the song on the radio, heading for the airport. No matter what happens, I've done it. Layla is safe and nothing else matters.

The traffic starts to get heavier and I find myself having to weave in and out of lanes to get through the traffic to the top of the queues.

We get to the stretch of carriageway close to the airport. It's only a half-mile away. I see the flashing sirens of police on the opposite side of the carriageway heading towards us. They are so small I can't make out the car shapes but I see them driving over the divide in the road, stopping on the road ahead of us. They're setting up to block me.

My foot comes off the accelerator slightly as my initial reaction.

I press it back down hard. The pursuing cars start to back off, realising my intentions. The two cars parked up ahead get closer and closer. The cops inside scramble to get out of them once they see me getting real close, not slowing down. I aim for right down the middle of both cars. The cops will just get clear whenever I make contact.

I smash through the small gap in the middle of both cars. I hit one, sending me into and bouncing off the other.

The engine chokes a little, forcing me to downshift the gears before picking up speed again. I continue on down the road, looking through the cracks in the windscreen that have come off from the collision. I hear a clunking coming from either the engine or the wheels but I don't concern myself too much about it. The airport entrance is just up ahead.

I see the cops clearing a gap in the road behind me, letting the pursuing cars through. I turn into the airport.

I drive right up to the entrance of the airport and park in one of the taxi drop-off points.

I get out of the car and abandon it, running into the airport as the growing sound of sirens descends on the grounds.

I enter the hustle and bustle of the airport. The place is packed full of people already dressed for their holidays. Shorts, t-shirts and some even wearing sunglasses even though there isn't a glimpse of the sun outside and in here is even darker.

I make my way across the sparkling white floor to the check-in desk. I open up my emails on my phone and show my ticket to the woman at the desk. She keys in my information on her computer and confirms the details.

She hands me a ticket and tells me to make my way to Gate Five. I leave the desk and start walking towards the escalator. I keep checking back over my shoulder at the entrance.

Eventually, when I'm on the escalator amongst other passengers, I see uniformed cops storm into the airport. I push my way up through the crowd on the escalator, getting to the top as fast as I can. I look down once I am at the top to see the cops running in my direction. I turn and start running.

I am forced to a stop when I get to the customs part, the part of the journey when you have to go through a metal detector. The queue is enormous but I have no choice but to stop and join up from the back. I hope for the queue to filter through quickly but it is a very slow process and I know the cops are gaining ground for every second I waste standing here. One more passenger gets through but I still can't see the metal detector from back here, there are too many bodies in front of me.

Out of patience, I start to push my way to the front of the crowd to the grunts and protests of others in the queue.

235

I almost get to the front when I hear someone shout from behind me.

'Hey! Stop that guy! The guy in the suit!' a cop shouts.

I look around, noticing that everyone has started backing off and all eyes have now turned on me.

One of the customs officers comes through the metal detector and grabs my sleeve, I shake him off and push him into the crowd. Two other custom guards try to stop me getting through the metal detector as I rush through but I break free from their clutches and run like hell. I manage to put some distance between myself and the cops. I get out of sight and try to get lost in the crowds around the nearby stalls, shops and cafeteria.

No matter where in the crowd I hide, I know I must stick out like a sore thumb.

I'm the only one around here in a suit. I take off my blazer and leave it by the entrance to one of the shops. I loosen off my tie and let it fall to my feet to get trampled on by those following behind me. I start looking around for something, a disguise of some sort.

Looking over to the seating area of the cafeteria, I notice someone has left their backpack and jumper on one of the seats. I weave my way through the crowd towards it. I casually stop beside it, pretending to look around for someone. I look to see if anyone is watching and sneakily pick up the jumper and walk on. It's a good fit when I throw it on on my way to the terminals. I follow the signs for 'Gate Five'.

An announcement comes over the speakers.

'Last call for passengers on Gate Five, Belfast to Glasgow.'

Knowing my window was closing, I start to hurry, pushing my way through the slow-moving crowds.

I hear someone shout from somewhere behind me, 'Police! Stop!'

I don't stop to look back, I break into a run, knocking a man over just to get past. The pain returns to my leg. Great timing for it. I know they are right behind me.

I force myself through the pain and I run what seems like halfway across the airport. People shout and scream as I storm past with the police at my back.

There are even a few wannabe heroes who step out into my path to catch me but I fight my way past them, either by charging them or throwing them to one side. I'm nearly there, the signs for Gate Five show that it is just around this corner. I feel a large bang against my right shoulder and the next thing I know, I'm on the ground. I'd completely missed a security guard standing amongst the crowd. He holds me on the floor as I struggle to get free. I turn my head to look back down behind me.

The cops are just about to get me, I see the closest one taking out a pair of handcuffs. I use all of my strength to shift the guard off me, I manage to catch him by surprise and he stumbles off balance.

I waste no time getting onto all fours, a sturdy position by the time he launches back onto me. I wrestle with him until I get back to my feet before throwing him against the wall, holding him against it. He puts both of his hands around my throat, squeezing so hard that it becomes difficult to breathe. I notice a collection of keys hanging from his trousers. I grab them, tugging them off and driving them into his thigh. He lets go in pain and crumbles to the floor as I rush around the corner and into the gate for the plane. I stop outside of it, the attendants turn, about to close it but I hesitate.

It's the last gate, the only gate here.

The cops will know where to look, I'm cornered. Noticing a sign on the ceiling, I go to the door under one of its arrows, the toilets. I go through and into the disabled toilet. It'll buy me a few seconds at least if they come in here. I lock the door and press my ear to it to listen.

Everything is silent, no commotion at all, then I feel a rumbling on my leg, a vibration.

I take out my phone to see that Colin is calling me, it's a video call.

What does he want? I answer, seeing his face appearing on the screen.

'Michael! Where are you, you fucking rat?'

'Me? I'm on my way out the country, nice knowing ya,' I say, looking away from the phone, listening to chatter beyond the door.

'You killed a man at his own son's funeral.'

'Don't get involved, Colin.'

'Too late, Michael. We're coming for you. We're coming for you, your family, everyone.'

'Colin, don't jump into this, think about it for a minute. Don't bring my family into this.'

'Fuck you,' he says before the screen goes black.

I feel a banging against my back, a banging on the toilet door.

'Open up!' I hear a voice shout.

The adrenaline comes back.

I go over to the toilet and stand on top of it to reach the handle of a small window. It's very stiff. I swing all of my weight on it as the door bangs again, so fiercely that I fear that it might break open.

'Police!' a man shouts.

I swing on the handle even harder now and it moves. I open the long, narrow window and lift myself up and out

238

of it. It's a very tight squeeze but I force myself through it, ripping a part of my trousers that gets caught on the jagged edge of the window sill.

I stand up and hear the lock breaking off the toilet door, I see figures rushing into the toilet below and I turn and start running again. I run across the rooftops of the airport, changing levels almost every fifty yards, the roof's surface is smooth and spongy, a quite odd feeling.

I start to look for a way off, an enclosed area of any sort.

I start heading east on the roof and come across a series of lower rooftops.

Among them, I find a gap, an alley of some description. I try to judge the drop, too high to fall from without injuring myself. I walk along the edge, trying to find anything to help me down. I come across a metal drainage pipe that runs the whole way from the roof to the ground from the guttering. I hang one of my legs over and boot it to test its sturdiness. It's rock solid.

I adjust myself and start to lower my legs down and around the pipe, my hands soon follow after letting go of the safety of the roof's surface. I slowly walk down the wall of the building, the whole way to the ground which is covered by overgrown thorns and nettles.

I drop the last few feet into the nettles, getting entangled in them. I fight my way out of them and get out of the alley, coming out onto a small access road. I look around. Shutters line the side of the building, this must be a goods-in area. I follow the road which takes me around to the large car park.

I get off the road and climb over the fence into the car park. I walk to the far end of the car park, the furthest point away from everything. I take off the jumper and wrap my right hand in it.

I pick out a small red car and punch in the driver's window.

The glass smashes in onto the car seat, with some of the glass falling by my feet. Reaching inside, I pop open the door and wipe the glass off the seat and out of the car. I get in and break off the plastic panel underneath the steering wheel and hot-wire it.

The engine kicks into life and I shut the door.

All of my instincts tell me to get out as quickly as I can but I get lost in thought at the wheel.

I'm left with the same predicament I had when Layla first went missing.

My family is still in danger. I can't leave here until I know they will be safe. I want to go straight down there and take them all out but I'm up against a small army, the odds are too much. I start to exhaust my ideas, my mind jumps from getting a gun, hiding my family and even getting Colin in his sleep.

They know I will be coming, Colin's not dumb, he knows me.

I need backup but there's no-one that has my back, I've nothing to offer. But, maybe it's not what I can offer, but rather what there is to be gained.

I know exactly where to go.

I finally let off the handbrake and drive slowly out of the car park. I come around the front of the airport and I start to see the flashing lights of the police cars and vans that occupy most of the entrance of the airport. I filter out in the light traffic leaving the grounds. I pass a large group of cops on the footpath but they don't even give me a second look. I get outside the grounds of the airport and disappear into the traffic bound for Belfast.

***

I drive to the bar which still has the scorch marks of my work outside its doors and on the road. I get out of the car and walk inside with no fear.

I go inside, past the young girl working there who is more interested in her phone than her customers. It's only after I pass her, going into the back that she takes notice of me, shouting after me.

I walk to the back rooms, turning into a small office.

Behind an old wooden desk and a computer is sat, Willy.

He braces in his seat when he sees me.

'What do you want?' he asks.

'I want you to set up a new meet for me.'

'With who?'

'Ridley.'

'I heard that you and Carl killed Chester. Why would I do anything for you? Why would I trust you?'

'Ridley is a businessman from what I gathered. I can offer him everything I took, plus a lot more.'

'Yeah, doesn't quite convince me. These guys, myself included, wouldn't mind seeing your head on a pike.'

'I just want him to hear what I have to say. What can be gained? If he doesn't like it, you can do what you want with me.'

'You know what, I'll humour you then. Just so happens Ridley is in town, actually looking for you, so this is perfect.'

'Good, I'll wait in the bar, make the call.'

I go into the bar and ask the phone-obsessed girl for a vodka and orange.

I get my way through a few drinks when the door swings open and I hear them enter and turn watch them come in.

Ridley is in a dark suit with his light spiked hair remaining the same as before. I stay still, trying not to spook them with any sudden movements.

One of his guys sits down next to me, leaning on the bar and staring at me. I pay no attention to him. Then he places a gun on the bar in front of him. I look at him, waiting for him to say something but it is Ridley who speaks from somewhere off behind me.

'You wanted to talk, well here I am, talk.'

I get up off my seat at the bar and turn around. Ridley is sat at one of the tables surrounded by his men, they are occupying the entire bar.

I take my drink and walk slowly over to the table and take a seat opposite him.

'Yeah that's right, I want to make a proposition,' I tell him.

'And what would that be?' he asks.

'Me and my brother have caused you a lot of trouble, cost you a lot of money. I think we can come to an arrangement that benefits us both with you taking all of the spoils.'

'Well, forgive me if I seem a bit reluctant but what is your proposal?'

242

'You got back a good chunk of what we stole from you when you came to our parents' house before burning it down, but me and my brother still managed to make sixty grand on the coke.'

'Still a bit short of the hundred and twenty you put me out of in the first place.'

'True but I can give you that sixty grand plus a further quarter mill.'

'How can you do that?' he asks surprised, his eyebrows raising.

'A former boss of mine, Tommy Bray, he had a rainy day fund. Only a few of us knew about it. It's buried in the warehouse he uses as a drug lab. I know where they will have it stored and when to hit it.'

'And what do you gain from all of this despite maybe a pardon from me?'

'I just want the leftovers of the new ring leader.'

**

It's ten o'clock and I stand watching the pouring rain from the shelter of the overhead motorway at the roundabout. A black van comes by and starts to slow down, eventually coming to a stop, the driver studying me thoroughly. The side door slides open to reveal a group of masked men inside.

'Get in!' one of the men shout at me.

I walk over and climb inside and the door slides shut again.

The inside falls completely pitch black, I feel the van race off again. I almost lose my balance but I put a hand out to catch myself against the van's wall. I find a spot on the floor to sit among the rest of the men.

The journey and the rocking of the van is enough to make anybody car sick. I do my best to hold it in, sometimes on the verge of retching.

I have to put up with the bumps and rocks of the chassis the whole way to Dublin.

The trip takes longer than I remember from back here, time has really slowed down.

All I have to look at is the faces of Ridley's squad. All dressed tactically.

Each of them with an automatic rifle, I never knew that this is what me and Carl were getting into, these guys look like trained killers.

There is no conversation between them, only the metallic shifting sounds of the van. I start hearing a slight rattle on the sides and on the roof of the van, then I catch on to it being rain from outside. I feel the van slowing down, Ridley looks in from the front seat.

'We're close. Get ready.'

The van comes to a halt. Everyone is silent and still.

'OK, go!' the driver shouts, bouncing out of the van along with Ridley.

The men in the back with me get up and move to the rear doors of the van. They swing them open and the guys start to jump out. I'm at the back of the queue, waiting for my turn to get out. As the last of them jumps out ahead of me, he stops me from getting out, putting his hands on the door of the van.

'No, you stay here. Boss' orders.'

'You don't know where to look,' I tell him, my knowledge being my bargaining chip.

244

'We'll come back for you,' he says before slamming the doors shut again, leaving me in darkness.

I wait in the van for five minutes, but that is my limit.

I get out of the van and hear the faint bursts of gunfire from inside the warehouse.

I go inside through a side door.

The warehouse floor has been converted into a make-shift drug operation. It covers the entirety of the space on the ground floor. Bodies lay scattered around the floor in the aftermath of a gunfight. I hear the blasts of gunfire coming from the offices. I go through a door and climb a staircase to get up to them.

I get to the top of the stairs and can see Ridley and his men ahead through the glass wall of the offices. A man launches on me from out of the darkness. He falls onto me, holding onto my arm to keep himself up. He doesn't say anything. He just looks at me hopelessly as he clings onto life. His bloodied hands start to lose their grip and his breathing becomes faint.

I shake the guy off my arm and go into the room after the last blast of gunfire.

The room is a complete mess, papers and folders lay scattered around. The glass walls of a neighbouring office lie shattered on the floor and I count at least three men laid out and still. Ridley's men continue to carefully stalk the room and check the bodies as Ridley enters the room from behind me. I run to the man closest to me that is face down on the floor. I roll him onto his back, it's not Colin. I look over towards the other two bodies when Ridley grabs my arm.

'Where is it hid?'

'Colin? Where is he?' I ask, confused.

245

I hear guns cock and reload before they draw on me.

'Where is it?' Ridley shouts.

'Ground floor toilets. Under the floor tiles.' I tell him.

Ridley and his men go downstairs and I go over to the next body.

I roll him onto his stomach, but he is dead too.

I hear the man next to us start to cough and I rush straight over to him.

'Where's Colin?' I interrogate.

'He's not here,' he tells me.

'Where then?'

'North. He said he might not be able to get to you but he can get to your family.'

'When did he leave?'

'Uh, um. About fifteen, twenty minutes before you guys showed up.'

I shove the man back down on the floor and run out of the room. I navigate the stairs, skipping the last seven steps by jumping them and running out of a fire escape.

I come out into the dark, cold Dublin air and start to race through ideas of how to get back to Belfast. Running around to the front of the building, I find that Ridley has left the van unguarded. I go for the driver's door and pull the handle but it won't open. I try to punch in the glass but it's thicker than most windows, it just won't break.

I punch and kick the door out of frustration, turning in my anger to bash off the wing mirror.

I leave the grounds of the warehouse and go out onto the footpath beside the busy road.

The intensity of the sheer number of headlights is almost blinding. I start slowly walking down the footpath beside the road, waiting impatiently for the traffic to ease to isolate one or two cars, to make them vulnerable to hijack. But the traffic doesn't ease.

I go to take a step onto the road but a van quickly changes lanes and sounds its horn loudly at me, almost hitting me before I retreat back to the safety of the footpath.

I stop walking, I'm not getting anywhere by going further and further down the road. I can see the headlights for miles down this stretch of road, I'm wasting time.

I contemplate going back to the warehouse for a moment, maybe Ridley will give me the key, but that's his getaway. Our deal came to an end in that office.

Fuck it, I think to myself. I find the slightest of gaps in the traffic and run out into the middle of the road. The sound of numerous horns sounding and tires screeching follow my path.

The dizzying headlights swerve to narrowly avoid me, the cars start to collide and crash into the sides of the road. I quickly sidestep to avoid being run down by one, only to be thrown onto the bonnet of another. I'm thrown up on the bonnet and crash, shoulder first, into the windscreen, cracking it. I quickly regain myself. Looking over the roof of the car, I can see that traffic has finally come to a stand-still behind. I climb down off the car as the driver gets out to check on me.

'Are you OK? Are you hurt?' he asks concerned.

I hold my shoulder, slumping down and disguising myself as weak, walking up to him.

'My shoulder, I think it's broken, I think my shoulder's broken.'

'I'll call an ambulance,' he says, getting his phone out.

As he puts the phone to his head, I shove him out of the way and into the side of a stationary car, getting into the driving seat of his car and speeding off.

***

I drive at ridiculous speeds, speeds that would normally scare me on my way back to Belfast. I look at the time on the dash, it's ten to midnight. I need to catch up to Colin, he already has a good head start on me.

I try to call Lisa to warn her, to tell her to take her mum and Layla and get out but she doesn't pick up, no matter how many times I call. I leave a message that I don't think will ever be heard.

The rain returns with a vengeance.

It becomes so intense that I'm struggling to see the white lines in the middle of the road, with my only navigation being the taillights that I come up on. The car starts to slip and slide on the road that is becoming quite flooded.

The rain hits the windscreen with such ferocity that it takes on the essence of an animal.

Soon, the street lights and the road ahead become familiar territory, the same stretches of road I've travelled on a thousand times, I'm back in Belfast.

The rain doesn't let up, not for a second. It still has me on edge, my heart beats so hard that I feel it wanting to break free of my chest.

Just as I pass the Belfast welcome sign, a car slides into the lane in front of me without warning or indication. I

248

have no time to react, no time to reach the brake before I slam into the back of it.

The collision sends me sliding into the central divider. I slam against the dash first and then the door, the window smashes in with most of the glass spreading over and resting on my lap before I grind to a halt.

It takes me a minute to take everything in.

I look back up the road through the window of the passenger seat. I can see the other car resting in the middle of the road. The headlights still shining and the windscreen wipers going crazy.

The driver door opens and I see a figure stepping out. I've gotta get back on the road, now. I reach for the key to turn the engine back on but a searing pain in my arm stops that from happening. I pull down on the collar of my t-shirt to look underneath at my shoulder.

All I can see is a darkened colour of what must be blood, covering my skin from the shoulder. I put my hand down under my jacket to feel my arm but snap my hand back as soon as it makes contact.

It's definitely broken.

I breathe heavily for a few seconds until the pain subsides.

I sweep away the glass and rest my right forearm on my lap. I awkwardly lean over to turn the key with my left hand, starting the engine. I use my left arm to do everything. Gears and steering wheel, I start driving one-handed.

Ten past one, I'm nearly there, is it quick enough? Even with only being streets away, I still race the car as if I only have seconds to spare. Then I pull into the street.

My breathing becomes more deep and rapid as I come up the street and Lisa's mum's house is slowly revealed from behind a curve in the road.

That's when I see a car parked right outside the house with its doors still opened.

My worst fears start to occupy my mind. I brake right outside the house and rush out of the car.

Gunshot after gunshot echoes throughout the street, a deafening series of blasts that come from inside the house.

I run across the grass and into the house.

The front door is wide open and there are some lights on inside. I go in, unarmed.

All is silent, I slowly place my first step inside the hall, listening carefully for any sound before the other foot follows. I want to shout out for Layla but I need to find out where they are first.

I carefully walk up the hall, then I see a pair of feet that lay on the floor, coming out from the living room. I slowly edge around the corner but no one is there.

I look at the man on the floor, it's one of Colin's guys. I continue on into the living room.

A pool of blood soaks the carpet where another man lays flat on his back, gunshots in his chest. I hear whimpering coming from the kitchen, weak, scared whimpers but I can't decide who they are coming from.

Then a loud, single gunshot goes off from inside the kitchen.

I brace myself for what I might find beyond the door leading to the kitchen.

I take a gun from the dead man on the carpet and I go to the kitchen door that is slightly ajar with whimpering

250

coming from the other side. I raise my gun up and swing open the door.

The whimpers continue, the first thing I notice is something by my feet. I look down to see the dressy shoes of the man laid face down in front of me. Looking up, I can't find the source of the whimpers, they are coming from under the kitchen table which has a cover draped over it. The cover has three small holes in it, bullet holes I would guess.

I turn my attention back to the man at my feet.

I take aim down at him and use one of my feet to turn him over. When I turn him over, I see the face of a former mentor, friend and foe.

It's Colin.

Someone has caught him right in the forehead.

I take my foot off him and aim at the kitchen table.

'Who's down there?' I shout, advancing on the table.

'Michael?' I hear a voice shout back.

A hand cups the bottom of the table cover and lifts it up to reveal that the sources of the whimpers came from Lisa.

Her eyes are red from tears, her lips still trembling.

'Lisa? How did —,' I lose my words in the confusion, how did Lisa take out Colin and two of his guys? Then I see someone else under the table.

I duck down to see a bloodied hand still gripping a pistol, his frame slumped against the wall at his back.

Carl looks back and me and smiles.

Blood starts dripping from his mouth and then he starts coughing. I get down and crawl underneath the table and sit beside him. One of his hands is resting on his bloody stomach. I look up to Lisa who is looking down on us.

'Where is Layla?' I ask her, concerned.

'She's upstairs with my mum, she's OK.'

I turn my attention back to Carl. I lift his hand off his stomach. He winces and I see a messy bullet wound. I put my good hand on his stomach, keeping pressure on it. All of our attentions turn to the door of the kitchen when we start to hear sirens getting close.

'Go on, get going,' Carl tells me.

'I'm not running any more,' I tell him.

Lisa has a worried look on her face, I know she is thinking the same as Carl before she speaks.

'He's right. You need to go,' she says quietly.

'I'm not going anywhere. I'm staying right here.'

Carl smiles at me and places his hand on top of mine on his stomach. Lisa kneels down and watches us. We all stay together until the colours of the police sirens flash in the darkness of the living room beyond.

The End

ABOUT THE AUTHOR

Paul McCracken is a Northern Irish author from Belfast, Northern Ireland.

Paul originally got into writing after completing a short course in film making with the charity, The Prince's Trust. Having completed the course, the studio owner encouraged Paul to start writing his own material, screenplays. Paul would spend the next few years learning the craft and eventually got into the quarter-finals of a screenplay competition based out of Los Angeles.

He badly wanted to get his work out into the public eye, with the prospect of getting a screenplay sold or made being very slim. Paul decided to start writing novels, focusing on the crime genre.

This is Paul's first published book.

It would go a long way if you could leave a review of this book on Amazon to help boost its ranking.

Printed in Great Britain
by Amazon